D. M. Thomas was born in Cornwall in 1935. His recent publications include his *Collected Poems* and translations of Pushkin. His previous novel *The White Hotel* was an international bestseller and has been translated into fourteen languages. *Ararat* is his fourth novel.

'Wonderfully powerful and impressive' *The Times*

'Thomas has written this fascinating work in response to the enormous success of *The White Hotel*. It's a novel for the '80s – explosiveness subdued in a dazzling, perplexing, controlled structure that will please all readers who admire Thomas' writing brilliance' *Publishers Weekly*

D. M. Thomas

ARARAT

SPHERE BOOKS LTD
Published by the Penguin Group
27 Wrights Lane, London W8 5TZ, England
Viking Penguin Inc., 40 West 23rd Street, New York, New York 10010, USA
Penguin Books Australia Ltd, Ringwood, Victoria, Australia
Penguin Books Canada Ltd, 2801 John Street, Markham, Ontario, Canada L3R 1B4
Penguin Books (NZ) Ltd, 182–190 Wairau Road, Auckland 10, New Zealand

Penguin Books Ltd, Registered Offices: Harmondsworth, Middlesex, England

First published in Great Britain by
Victor Gollancz Ltd 1983
Published in Abacus by
Sphere Books Ltd 1984
27 Wrights Lane, London W8 5TZ
Copyright © D. M. Thomas 1983
Reprinted 1984 (twice), 1988

Reproduced, printed and bound in Great Britain by
Hazell Watson & Viney Limited
Member of BPCC plc
Aylesbury Bucks

To. A. L.

· AUTHOR'S NOTE ·

Pages 51–68 are a translation by the author of Pushkin's narrative fragment *Egyptian Nights* (1835); the continuations of the narrative (pp. 80–115 and 116–121) are the author's invention. Blok's poem "Night, the street, a lamp, the chemist's . . ." (p. 78) is translated by Avril Pyman in her *Life of Aleksandr Blok*, vol. II (London and New York: Oxford University Press, 1980), and his poem "Steps of the Commander" (pp. 31–2) is translated by the author. The quotations on pp. 179–183 from the Armenian poet Nareg (Krikor Naregatsi, 951–1003) are from his *Book of Lamentations*; these, and the epigraph from Kevork Emin (p. 19), are translated by Diana der Hovanessian and Marzbed Margossian in their *Anthology of Armenian Poetry* (New York: Columbia University Press, 1978). The principal source for factual details relating to the Armenian massacres and diaspora is Christopher J. Walker's *Armenia: The Survival of a Nation* (London: Croom Helm, 1980).

D.M.T.

· Contents ·

P·R·O·L·O·G·U·E

SERGEI ROZANOV HAD MADE AN UNNECESSARY JOURNEY from Moscow to Gorky, simply in order to sleep with a young blind woman. The woman, who turned out to be not so young, and who had dreadfully thin legs which had not been apparent in the photograph she had sent him, came from Kazan; Gorky had seemed a convenient mid-point for their first rendezvous. She was studying for her doctorate at the University, and was writing a thesis on Rozanov's poetry. She had written to him, and they had spoken by phone. Rozanov had liked her voice, but above all it was her blindness which had appealed to him. He had never slept with a blind woman. Although she was married, it had not been too difficult to persuade her to this encounter.

It had not worked out as he had hoped. Her gnarled, veined hands told him that she could not be many years younger than he – Rozanov was fifty. It was ludicrous to be studying for a doctorate at that age. He took her thin legs as an affront. But above all her blindness, when he came face to face with it, did not at all attract him. He found her wandering, unattached pupils creepy. He was glad when they had finished dinner and were in the outrageously expensive hotel bedroom and the light could be turned out.

What appalled him more than anything was that he knew Kolasky was in Moscow, on leave from his tank unit on the western front, and Rozanov's absence (supposedly to lecture on Maxim Gorky) gave the major general a free rein with Rozanov's mistress, Sonia. Sergei believed his mistress was only playing with Kolasky, using him as blackmail to force Sergei to do something about his domestic situation; but he could not be quite sure. Where Sonia was concerned, he was not quite sure of anything. Yet stupidly he had opened up a night in which they could dine, talk, laugh, and make love.

Rozanov shivered at the thought, and barely stopped himself from ringing her, even in Olga's presence.

Olga's love-making was acrobatic but lacking in finesse. She seemed to think it was enough to whisper constantly that she loved him. Eventually he had to move apart from her and finish it off himself. She begged him to tell her what she was doing wrong, and of what he was thinking. His reply – "I'm thinking about the Decembrists" – added to her confusion. He did not enlighten her, but went on staring at the fluttering curtains in the darkness.

"I'm afraid I wasn't very good for you," the woman said sadly. "I'm not very experienced."

"You were fine. I liked it so much I kept holding back. I held back too long." He tried to think of an excuse for getting dressed and leaving her there, with money to pay the bill, but there was nowhere to go. The Sakharovs were somewhere in Gorky, but they would not thank him for turning up at their door at midnight. Besides, they were watched; it could only bring trouble.

No, he would have to see the meeting through to the bitter end, and take the first flight home. The oblivion of sleep would have been a mercy, but unfortunately sleep would not come to him. Torrential rain lashed the window; a storm wind made the jerry-built hotel shake. The storm had arisen during the evening; tomorrow he would find the autumn trees stripped bare. The blind woman was of course glad he was wakeful. She wished to make the most of every moment.

It was like trying to sleep in the ark, Sergei reflected. In his mind's eye he saw Ararat, although he had never been to Armenia. His mother had been born there, and consequently it gripped his imagination; he feared to exchange his vision for reality. With the pleasant and intelligent, but boring, stranger, Rozanov lay in Gorky and thought of Ararat. Two by two they went into the ark. . . .

The conversation in the dark had taken a serious, academic turn. He felt exquisitely bored by her profound analysis of his recent verse. After a while he stopped listening, and listened only to the wind and the rain. Embracing him tightly, aware of his silent mood, Olga asked him if he would improvise a story for her. She had heard of his talent for improvisation. He had inherited the skill from his Armenian grandfather: a man who, having in his youth witnessed an atrocity and developed a stammer, cured it by roaming the remote regions of Armenia, telling stories at isolated villages. He had perished, alongside the poets Varoujan and Siamanto, in the genocide of 1915.

"Okay," Rozanov said, after she had repeated her plea that he improvise for her. It would be·less tedious than having to carry on a serious conversation. "You'll have to give me a theme."

"Can't you make one up yourself?"

"No, it has to come from you."

Olga meditated. "Improvisations," she said: "that's your theme."

He chuckled. "That reminds me of *Egyptian Nights*."

"I didn't know you'd been to Egypt, Sergei," she said. "When? Pre-Sadat?"

"No!" He chuckled again, though his mind flashed to the carnage he had seen recently on the television news. "I meant Pushkin's story."

"Oh, I see! You must think me terribly ignorant. I don't think it's in braille."

"Really? Then we must put that to rights, Olga. It's wonderful! He wrote it, or rather began it, after hearing Mickiewicz deliver an impromptu poem, which overwhelmed him. Mickiewicz must have been fucking good to have overwhelmed Pushkin. I guess he must have been the greatest *improvisatore*."

"From what I've heard, he couldn't have been better than you."

"That's nonsense. It's just a game, like doing crosswords. To make anything half decent, I have to slave away like everyone else."

"Well, make it a long improvisation, please. Till the dawn that never comes . . . Will it be a *povest'* or a poem?"

"Who knows? I'll have to sit in the armchair, if you don't mind. . . . 'Improvisations'. . . that's an interesting theme. Give me a few minutes to collect my thoughts. Do you want some more wine?"

"No, darling: you have some more . . . I've had enough."

Rozanov got out of bed with relief, found his dressing-gown and wrapped it round him, curled up in the chair, closed his eyes, and concentrated. . . .

"Three writers thrown together by chance," Rozanov began, "sat up talking and drinking in a hotel on a sultry October night. Before they split up after midnight they agreed, at the drunken insistence of one of their number, to improvise on a common theme, and to compare results the following day, before the commencement of the congress which they were attending.

"The American woman, a writer of romantic fiction, was clearly at a disadvantage; she did not feel committed to fulfilling a promise extracted under duress, and in any case she thought such game-playing childish. The Russian poet had a reputation for facility, but was drunk. The Armenian was still sober, and moreover was a traditional story-teller: his proud skill had been challenged by a disreputable Muscovite.

"The subject chosen for their improvisation slept serenely through the night. It did not dream of a beloved, dead, ice-cold Armenian father, as the American woman did. It did not fight demons, as the Soviet poet seemed to be doing, for a time at least. It did not talk softly, as the Armenian story-teller did. It did not dream of Noah's flood, nor of the more terrible flood of 1915. It stood. It let the storm clouds improvise around it. . . ."

N·I·G·H·T

And you, my mountain,
Will you never walk toward me?
KEVORK EMIN

O·N·E

MY DOCTOR HAS FORBIDDEN ME DEPRESSION. IT WAS SHE who, knowing I was to visit Armenia by way of America, persuaded me to cancel my air tickets and take this sea voyage. "You need complete calm."

It was the first time she had visited me at home. Her quick eyes took in everything: the wall of birches beyond the window; the fragment of Siberian meteorite on my filing cabinet; my desk with a white sheet of paper still in the typewriter; above it, a sketch of Blok at the first night of *Carmen*; the clay unicorn and *rusalka* on the ebony chest to the right of my divan bed. "Why are you so obsessed with sex?" she asked, gazing at my seventeenth-century ikon. She is full of curiosity — it is why I go to her.

"Because I spewed up milk into my mother's lap when I was two," I said. "People were starving, so she stuffed me too full. I still hate milk."

She nodded, with complete understanding. "You

should rest," she said. My bed was covered with papers. "I can't," I replied. "A writer can't enjoy sickness. These are proofs of a new edition of Pushkin's stories — I have to correct them by Thursday. Also I have to read, and write reports on, these books." I pointed to a couple of American novels, lying on the bed near the latest issue of *Novy Mir*.

"Why? For whom?"

I shrugged. "They like to keep a check on what's being written about us over there. . . . One is a detective story set in Moscow! Would you believe it! Can't you see it in *Pravda*? – '*Poirot Investigates Meyerhold's Murder.*'" I laughed weakly and derisively. I reached down beside the bed. My half-crippled cleaning lady had left me a thermos of soup and some cans of beer before hobbling off home. I picked up a can, wrenched off the seal, and gulped.

"How do you feel?" my doctor asked. "What's the matter?" She perched on the bed and I caught a faint scent of freshly washed hair. It is long, straight, and the colour of lemons — her crowning glory, though I noticed some streaks of grey.

"I don't know. I was hoping you'd tell me. I'm burning up, or shaking with cold. I'm swimming in sweat."

She took my pulse, but her gaze drifted away to a faded water-colour of a blond Georgian girl I had loved for four days, ten years ago; she lost track of the time. She is not very knowledgeable or skilful – but curious. "You have a fever, Surkov," she observed. "How are your problems?"

"I'm terribly locked in myself. So tightly locked that sometimes I can hear of a whole planeful of people being killed – or a friend telling me he's got cancer – or a dissident being arrested – without feeling; even with a slight *frisson* of excited pleasure. Other times, I can't help being others, I can't help becoming others. Everyone, everything. Not a sparrow falls without my knowing about it, and suffering its death."

"Ah, that's from the Bible!" she said, smiling.

"Yes!"

"I could give you tranquillizers, but it's not really an answer, is it?"

We were silent, looking at each other helplessly.

I saw her eyes flick aside to the unicorn. "Do you like it?" I asked. "I bought it not long ago on a trip to Rumania, but the unicorn is really an Armenian creature, like the raven and the dove. Did you know he was the only animal who wouldn't go in the ark? He stayed outside and swam! I can't remember if he survived or drowned. But you can't help admiring him, can you? Telling Noah to get lost! He's company for the *rusalka* I bought in the Crimea, a couple of years ago. She reminds me of my mother, actually. Sturdy and short. But why do you think she's got her hand resting in her lap like that, palm up? No, I don't know either. Maybe she feels more vulnerable, having come out of the sea? She's covering it but looks inviting too, don't you think? I'd really love to visit Armenia. Break away from all this. But I don't think I could stand its mountain stoniness, its heat, its purity, yet. I'll go there by way of New York."

I paused to take a breath; I'd been speaking quite rapidly. I picked up my can of beer from the floor and drained it. I don't normally like beer, but just lately beer, straight from the fridge, has become a kind of religion. I take another cigarette. My doctor's response to my smoking has always been to encourage it, or at least not to discourage it. Now, since I can't find my lighter in the jumble of bedclothes, she gets her matches from her handbag and lights my cigarette for me.

"I'll tell you an amazing story about the unicorn's head," I continued. "If you examine it – do you examine unicorns? – you'll see that the horn is removable. It fits into a hole. Well, one morning I happened to glance at it and I saw the horn wasn't there! I looked around for it – and where do you think it was? Resting between the thighs of the bathing girl! Its tip was in her hand! It had somehow got across to her in the night. I accepted it as a paranormal event. But then, just casually, I mentioned it to the cleaning lady who comes twice a week, and as cool as a cucumber she said she'd taken out the horn so she wouldn't damage it while dusting, and must have forgotten to put it back! Now, she's fiftyish, fat and breathless, a good soul but not very bright, happily married – a perfectly ordinary middle-aged woman. And she puts the horn just *there*, between her thighs – so it shouldn't get broken while she dusted! That's much more mysterious than telekinesis! Why did she do it? Can you explain it?"

"The menopause, being overweight."

But she looked shamefaced, as if she knew I knew she was guessing. A long silence. I searched for words to break it. "You see, now that I'm sick, Olga can't visit me. Or Irina, my own daughter. And in a way it's a relief. I'm not divided. And Zina is very good to me. But it's not healthy when a woman you've loved for twenty years can't come to see you when you're sick. And what will happen when I'm on my deathbed?"

"How old are you?" she asked.

"Seventy."

She looked at me compassionately. "You can't be much more than fifty. I think you should go into hospital."

"Oh no! You're not getting me into a *psikhushka*! I know all about them! Sulphur injections . . . they would *really* help my fever, wouldn't they? And trifluoperazine to deaden my mind and feelings . . ."

She laughed. "No, not a *psikhushka*! A very good nursing home!"

"Who would I name as my next of kin? Zina or Olga? My wife or my mistress? I know what's brought this on. It's *Zhivago*. It's the storm over the Nobel Prize. They want me to leave, and there's nothing I'd like more. I loathe this place. I have no connection with it. I want to get out, but I can't. Because I'd have to choose between Zina and Olga. I couldn't do that. I could only be happy if I took my unhappiness with me, but they wouldn't allow me that much luggage. I can only beg to be allowed to stay put, in a place I loathe."

My doctor spread her hands wide. "I don't think there's anything I can do for you."

"You can sleep with me," I said.

I saw I had struck again her sense of curiosity, her great – perhaps her only – strength as a doctor. "Why should you want me to do that?"

"Because of our one-sided relationship. I've been to your surgery countless times. You know almost all there is to know about me. I've poured out my problems, my confessions. You looked at my penis when I told you I was worried about the lump that came up when I had an erection. Though, admittedly, you saw it in its unerect state and so couldn't help. You looked at my anus when I had piles. But about you, I know nothing. You sit behind that desk, wrapped up tight in your woolly skirt and sweater."

"I should think you had more than enough of women," she said.

"But I want to know you. Is that so very wrong?"

"Won't your wife be home soon?"

"No, Vera Andreyevna's at Mosfilm; she doesn't get back till after seven. Even if she found us she wouldn't mind. She's very tolerant. It's the way she got me, after all."

"I can't believe she wouldn't mind." But all the same she had stepped out of her shoes and was peeling off her tights. I turned away. I hate their habit of shrivelling into baby's rompers – and that grotesque seam. When she lay beside me my fever created an oily film between us. I felt my lack of energy. I stayed limp. She was very understanding. "It's because you're sick and depressed," she said. I wanted to assure her it was not that I didn't find her desirable. "You have a beautiful cunt," I said, "and a tender little arsehole." She laughed. "So now we're on equal terms, you think?" "Not quite," I said. "I don't know your problems."

Getting out of bed and beginning to roll her tights on, she said, "It would take far too long."

· I ·

It was then she forbade me depression, and advised this voyage. It is a splendid white liner, and my cabin is pleasant. The beauty of it is that Zina and Olga are left behind, and my life is a blank page. There are many attractive women in the ship's dining room, but I shan't get involved. My doctor has been strict about that. "Fuck them if you must," she said; " if you can. But on no account become involved." And that fits in absolutely with how I feel.

Some of the young women are Olympic athletes, either returning home from the Moscow Games or travelling to take up scholarships in the United States in preparation for the Los Angeles Olympics. I contrive to sit opposite one of them at dinner. She is a slim boyish gymnast, called Anna, a Pole, who looks a little like Nadia Comaneci. But she tells me sadly that she slipped off the beam, and also made a hash of the asymmetric bars. Her best mark was an 8.2 in the floor exercises. She is determined to do better in Los Angeles. God knows how she has got hold of a visa, but good luck to her.

She asks me what I do for a living, and is surprised when I say that I'm an athlete too. "I'm really a sprinter," I explain, "but ten years ago I was requested – well, I didn't have much choice about it – to run a marathon. I found it dreadful but I staggered in. Although it was my first marathon, I finished it second. I started my second marathon before I'd finished the first, and I didn't do very well, though I was pleased with my performance. In my third marathon I came in first, yet it wasn't very satisfying. It made me realize, all the more, I'm really a sprinter. I shall run one more marathon – possibly 10,000 metres – then go back to the sprints."

I was, of course, teasing her, referring – respectively – to my life of Sholokhov, and my novels, *Envy* and *Leningrad Awakes!* But (possibly because her Russian wasn't up to following me anyway) she nodded as if she understood. Her thin, pale face could light up with a charming, mournful smile; but she became still and grave when I asked her if she thought we would move into her native land, and said sincerely that I hoped we wouldn't.

We are passing the coast of Denmark. It is dark, but the lights of some coastal town shine out clearly. I am on deck with Anna, and the spray blows cold and salty in our faces. She says she is missing her parents. I reply that she is lucky to have parents to miss. "My father died in the camps," I explain, "when I was not much older than you. He had been away all through the war, and fought bravely. He was back home for a few months; then – off to the Gulag. My mother lived on until about ten years ago; but she spent the last years of her life in a home. We call them homes because they're not. I couldn't have her living in Moscow with me because I spend every summer and autumn in the writers' colony at Peredelkino, outside the city; and at other times I'm away a lot. Also she would have hated the untidiness. I'm not a neat person." Spray drenched my face. I stopped speaking, aware that I was disobeying my doctor.

The young gymnast slid her arm through mine. In spite of her youth, I could see she felt sad for me, and I was touched by her sympathy. Glancing at her in the faint glow of the sea (there was no moon or stars), I saw how very young she was: probably no more than sixteen. Gymnasts are so very young.

It was a quiet night. The sea was calm for such a dangerous coast. Still, I was alarmed when she disengaged herself from me, took hold of the ship's rail with both hands, and lifted herself into a perfect handstand. But I could feel the absolute confidence in her strong arms: though they trembled. Her skirt falling away over her breast, I saw the faint gleam of white briefs; yet there was nothing erotic or provocative in her sudden action; rather, something innocent and schoolgirlish and high-spirited. She was, I realized, diverting me – cheering me up. After keeping her perfect balance for a minute or so, she slowly lowered herself to the deck. She breathed heavily, and laughed. "If only I could have done that in Moscow!" she said.

I was moved by her youth, the transience of her art. By the time the Los Angeles Games came round, she would be almost too old; her breasts would have rounded out. I touched her almost-absent breast. We kissed gently, and I persuaded her easily not to go to the disco but to my cabin. I hoped it would take me out of myself. I was terribly locked in my own skull; and – paradoxically – that gave me the feeling that my mind floated an inch or two above my head. Lately I've had that sensation a lot. When we entered my cabin she asked me not to turn on the light. Shivering in my arms she said, "I'm still a virgin." I apologized for hurting her. "I like it," she whispered. I whispered in return some tender lines of Akhmatova, since both her name and her fragility reminded me of her. I thanked her for sharing my lonely voyage. I grew strong and hard with the knowledge of being the first to take her. With a gasp, she tightened on me. I could see only the whites of her eyes, the occasional glimmer of her teeth as she smiled. I felt a paternal love and care for her – this forlorn child going to a strange country.

But when, in the light of dawn through the porthole, I awoke, feverish, hot, and pulled the sheet off us and looked at her sleeping form, I saw nothing had changed. The sharp shoulder-blades, the shape of her rib cage through the skin, the gap between her skinny thighs, filled me with pity for her but also relief. I wouldn't be able to make love to her again. I opened, and drained, a can of beer; smoked a cigarette; listened to the drone of the ship's engines; and watched Anna's trembling, dreaming eyelids. She was a sweet, attractive girl. Once I had explained to her that my doctor had forbidden involvement, there was no reason why we shouldn't be good friends on the voyage.

Smoking my second cigarette, drinking my second can

of beer, looking down at Anna, and thinking of Donna,
my pen friend in New York, I recalled Blok's "Steps of the
Commander" and I murmured it to myself. . . .

A thick and heavy curtain at the entrance,
    Behind the window – night's mist.
What price now your tedious freedom,
    Don Juan, knowing fear at last?

Cold and empty is the sumptuous bedroom,
    The servants sleep, the night is deaf.
From some blessed, unknown, distant country
    Comes the sound of cock-crow.

What can sounds of bliss mean to a traitor?
    The moments of life are numbered.
Donna Anna sleeps, her hands crossed on her heart,
    Donna Anna is dreaming. . .

Whose cruel features are reflected,
    Frozen, in the mirror?
Anna, Anna, is it sweet to sleep in the grave?
    Is it sweet to dream unearthly dreams?

Life is empty, senseless, and unfathomable!
    Go out to battle, ancient Fate!
And in reply – triumphant and enamoured –
    A horn sounds in the snowy darkness . . .

A black, silent motor car flies past,
    Like an owl, its lights splashing in the night.
With muffled, heavy footsteps the Commander
    Enters the house . . .

The door flies open. Out of the immense cold, a sound
  Like a clock striking hoarsely in the night –
A clock striking: "You asked me to supper.
  I have come. Are you ready? . . ."

To the cruel question there's no answer,
  No answer – only silence.
There is fear in the sumptuous bedroom at the hour
  of dawn,
  The servants are sleeping, and the night is pale.

At the hour of dawn it is cold and strange.
  At the hour of dawn the night is dim.
Maiden of Light! Where are you, Donna Anna?
  Anna! Anna! – Silence reigns.

Only in the fearful mist of morning
  The clock strikes for the last time:
Donna Anna will rise in the hour of your death.
  Anna will rise in the hour of death.

Only I did not quite reach the end of the poem, for I
must have whispered the words "Anna! Anna!" louder,
and she awoke. Startled, she asked me what was wrong. I
said, nothing, only that I had a fever, and perhaps she
should fetch the doctor. She kissed me anxiously on the
lips, and sprang out of bed. I saw again the bones beneath
the skin as she hooked on her skimpy white bra and pulled
on her white briefs, and felt relieved that I was going to be
left in peace. I felt irritated when she kissed me again,
hungrily, and said "I love you," before leaving. I wonder
if, in spite of myself, I have given her the wrong impression. And it is true that I burn up women as a marathon
runner burns up his flesh. How many had I had? Three

hundred? Three thousand? I needed the coming Revolution to cleanse my spirit. I needed to confess. The ship's doctor, when he turned up, did not invite intimacy; a Latvian, in his rimless spectacles resembling Lavrenti Beria, he had been blanched and scoured by arctic winds.

Nevertheless, I decided to be frank with him. Impassively he took my temperature, then, while he checked my pulse rate, asked me when I had first had this fever. I thought carefully before replying, in the German we both spoke badly:

"Very early in life. When I married Lyubov' Dmitriyevna, I made it clear our marriage would never be consummated, since I needed to sleep with whores, and to be able to worship her. Actually, we *did* consummate it – once only; a few years after the wedding. It seemed to us both that we should complete our knowledge of each other, just that one time. Lyubov' Dmitriyevna bores me; but I need her boredom. I can't write unless she's in the house; on the other hand, I would find it tedious to have to acknowledge her presence. She is an actress. It takes her away a good deal, and then I am not happy until she is back. Once, she came back and confessed that she had been unfaithful, and was pregnant. I was filled with joy to know that my Lyubov' had been impregnated by this unknown rival; and I felt joyful about the child, promising that I would regard it as my own offspring. But little Mitya died, after only ten days in this world. His meaningless life and death shattered me.

"I also love my mistress, Lyubov' Alexandrovna. She is an opera singer. She, too, bores me, but in a sexually obsessive way. I crave the boredom of her spasmodic sensuality. She has long red-gold hair. When I sit in the theatre watching her sing *Carmen*, the whole stage is dark except for the red-gold of her pubic hair that I literally can see moving about the stage, under her dress, corsets and petticoats.

"You may not know that Lyubov' means love.

"I love Love, and the child of Love, the love-child. I am in love with Love. Love is the centre of my life. Love acts, and Love sings. Love is the Most Beautiful Lady, and has a dark ambiguous cunt. I am the child of Love, and her master. Love fills my days with boredom, and gives my nights moments of rapture. Love is laying me waste, but I want her devastation. I love Love when she combs her red-gold hair, and when she whispers shameful phrases in the dark. I love her when I am sick, and she ministers to me. I love her when she presses the golden swan to her slim body; and when she broods tenderly over the Christ child. I love her when she sits naked on a rock, her hair in strands from the sea water, her left hand resting palm-upwards on her sturdy thighs — whether to give or to take, we don't know.

"And — yes — I am beginning to feel much better, doctor. I think I'd like to get up and dress."

Protesting that my temperature is dangerously high still, my doctor submits and helps me on with my shirt.

I think I can even take some breakfast. The ship is rolling heavily and I stagger into the dining room. Anna is sitting with a fat black discus-thrower from Cuba; she sees me and waves to me with a childlike openness of affection and surprised happiness. She is relieved to see me better. In the presence of the discus-thrower, it is impossible to tell her that I can't become involved with anyone; and when we are left alone, it's still not possible. I can see in her face that last night's spell is unbroken, and she clearly intends we shall pass the day together. I tell her I have to spend it working. It is true enough, in its way. But I can see she is disappointed and puzzled. Later I glimpse her at the swimming pool, where her white one-piece swimsuit accentuates her thinness. In contrast I am attracted (as last night I would have thought impossible) to the gross black girl, the discus-thrower. I imagine that mountain of flesh lowering itself on to me, and there is something perversely exciting about the thought. To be lost in so much flesh. I take it as a sign of returning health.

In the smoke-room, there is no one but an old man, who reads a book and looks sad. I say "old man," but maybe it is just his white hair and leathery skin. Perhaps he is not so old. I forget that my own hair is now quite grey. But I am surely not wrong about his sadness. He is only pretending to read his book. His eyes keep drifting towards me, and he obviously wants to talk. Well, I feel in a much more cheerful mood, and there is no harm in helping a fellow man in distress. Let him talk to me if he wants.

I remark on the pleasantly warm autumn weather, and it allows us to chat about the old-fashioned pleasures of ocean voyages. "Are you on holiday? What do you do for a living?" he asks, in a friendly way. "I'm a writer," I reply. "Really a poet; but in the last few years I've also written a biography and two novels. I've felt rather lonely, and writing a novel is a good way of making friends. One's life becomes increasingly fictional in middle age, I find. There's no longer a great difference between real life and fiction. . . . But that's a feature of our age generally, don't you think? Fiction seems tame compared with reality; and people's reality is so fantastic it seems like fiction. . . . Take the supposed memoirs of Shostakovich, for instance, which I've read in *samizdat*. Genuine or a forgery? Does it really matter? . . ."

I trail to a halt, conscious that I've rambled. But the old man is nodding, smiling. "Aren't you Victor Surkov?" he asks. "Yes, I thought so! I read about you in *Krokodil*. Hasn't your book won a Lenin Prize? Congratulations! I've forgotten the title of the book."

"*Leningrad Awakes!*"

"Ah, yes! I must read it. Is that the book you've got in your lap?"

I laugh. "No! This could hardly be published in the Soviet Union! At least, not the complete text."

He asks if he may glance at the book, and to save him getting up I carry it across to him. He reads the title, with lips that tremble slightly, the way old people's sometimes do when they read.

"Ah! . . . Babi Yar . . . I was there."

This last phrase falls with a sigh, like the fall of a birch leaf.

I mutter my sympathy. He looks ill; and I want to divert him from these tragic memories. "Where have you been living?" I ask.

"I am stateless."

I nod. "And what do you do – or what *did* you do?"

"I've been a soldier; and involved in international politics."

I nod again, encouragingly. He tells me his name is Finn; of Scandinavian origin. There is something Nordic about his form and features. He is on his way to deliver a speech at the United Nations. He asks me why I am on this voyage. I tell him about my American Armenian friend whom I have never met. His face becomes ashen. "I know Armenia well," he says. "I was there during the First World War."

"It's a terribly tragic country."

"Yes, and never more so than in 1915."

"Were you involved in the holocaust?"

He sighed deeply. "I was."

"Tell me about it — if it's not too distressing for you."

"It does distress me, but I'd like to tell you about it." He moved carefully, tottering a little, to a chair next to me, and settled himself in it. His teeth were badly decayed, and his eyes had a yellow tinge.

"It's difficult to know where to begin," he said. "For there was no precise beginning. I was a young army officer, serving at first in the Bulanik district, about 50 miles north-west of Moush. There had been some incidents of torture of Armenians during June — teeth knocked out, nails pulled out, limbs twisted, noses beaten down, the rape of wives and daughters in the presence of their menfolk — that sort of thing."

As Finn leaned forward I smelt his unpleasant breath. "It was of course necessary," he said, "to deport the Armenians from Turkey. But I have often wondered if we could have done it in some other way. We rounded up all the male villagers from around Moush on 10 July: herded them into concentration camps and bayoneted them. The women and children we drove into large wooden sheds and set fire to them. Of the 60,000 Armenians who had been living in Moush, very few survived.

"No, my memory is not as good as it used to be. Earlier

than that, we had moved against the inhabitants of Erzindjan. We told them they were being deported to Mesopotamia. Soon after we left the town, we separated the men from the others, and killed them. The women and children went on. Many were attacked in the early stages of their journey, and their clothes taken from them. When they reached the Kemakh gorge, overlooking the Euphrates, we tied their hands behind their backs. I gave the orders to pitch them over into the gorge. Probably 25,000 Armenians of Erzindjan were slaughtered, about half of them at the Kemakh gorge.

"Next we turned to the Armenians of Baiburt. We rounded up about 17,000. We couldn't prevent brigands from the hills swooping down, stealing their clothing and abducting the girls. The men had already been shot, just outside Baiburt. At the Kemakh gorge we disposed of the women and children in the usual way. Some of them tried to swim to the riverbanks, but we managed to shoot them. The same thing happened to the villagers from the plain of Erzerum.

"Next, I was ordered to go to Trebizond. Being near the coast, we were able to throw many people into the sea, or send them out in old boats and sink them. But many more were got rid of by forced marches. For us soldiers, there was hardly any respite. But I remember one day, I managed to go and bathe in the river Yel-Deyirmeni. It was rather shallow, and I saw a woman's nude body in the river. Her long hair floated down the current, her bloated white belly gleamed in the sun. I noticed that one of her breasts was cut off. I was therefore sure it was not the responsibility of my own troops. I saw other bodies, and a human arm caught up in the roots of a tree. The river became choked with bodies, like logs drifting down. Then I saw a long band of frothy blood clinging to the bank. I should guess we killed almost all of the 17,000 Armenians in the town of Trebizond. And when we marched the 18,000 Armenians of Kharput into the desert, only 150 got through. Some women drowned by flinging themselves into wells, so thirsty had they become, their tongues like charcoal. Yet in spite of those filthy bodies, the others still drank from the wells.

"Am I boring you?" he asked; for he had seen me glance at my watch. I explained that I was trying to cut down my smoking, and rationing myself to one every half an hour. But it was very difficult. "I know," he said. "I gave up smoking ten years ago, but I still dream now and then of smoking a cigarette. It's a dreadful addiction."

I suggested taking a stroll on deck, for the atmosphere in the smoke-room had become stale. But he was caught up in the story of his life, and – as if he had not heard me – continued:

"Mostly the men were killed locally, but the women and children struggled over steep mountain paths to the parched deserts. They were robbed of all they had, raped if they were attractive, and then killed. In the province of Dirarbekir we got rid of 570,000. An unbelievable figure, isn't it? But I assure you it is true. I have seen my own soldiers put up their hands to avert the sight of the bloated naked corpses of murdered women lying by the roadside, and in the desert wastes. In the plain of Maskinah, everywhere one looked there were little hills, each of which contained 200 to 300 corpses. Those who survived were racked by dysentery. I saw little children so hungry they ate anything they could find – grass, earth, even excrement. I saw women pick out the undigested oak kernels from horses' excrement. In Deir-ez-Zor I was ordered to inflict cruel punishments: bastinado, hanging, the rape of little girls. I was ordered to fling hundreds of Armenians into a deep hole in the ground. It must have been 150 feet deep. Those at the bottom soon died. Those at the top lived on for a few days.

"Yet altogether there has been great exaggeration of the numbers killed. It is certain that no more than a million were killed. I have heard it said there were a million and a half killed. This is not true."

The old man stopped speaking, exhausted. I took the chance to plead hunger, and a lunch appointment with a young lady. It was not true, but I wanted to get out into the open air. Fortunately the old man said he was not hungry. In fact I looked for Anna in the dining room, but her table was full. After I had eaten, I went to my cabin for a while. But I was given little chance to rest, for soon the ship's doctor appeared. The gross black discus-thrower was with him. Apparently she was training also as a nurse. She gave me some pills at the doctor's instruction. He repeated and emphasized my own doctor's instruction that I must not become depressed, but must enjoy the sea air.

After they had gone, I slept for a few hours; and when I awoke it was dark. Strolling on deck I came upon Finn. He came straight up to me and started to talk as if we had had no interruption. "In 1918," he said, "I was in Baku. I had orders to kill all the Armenians in the street. The whole of Surakhanskoi Street was covered with dead bodies of children not older than nine or ten. Many of them had had their throats cut, others had been bayoneted. I was obliged to drive my car over the dead children. The sound of crushing bones was appalling. The car wheels became covered with the intestines of dead bodies. Later, in Smyrna, I had orders to set fire to the Armenian quarters. Thousands of screaming people rushed to the dockside, hoping for rescue on the ships there, and were drowned. I actually saw one poor woman give birth to a baby as she was pushed over into the harbour."

Silently we fell into step.

"You said you were at Babi Yar," I observed quietly.

"Yes. Again, it was necessary to get rid of the Jews, but if I had my time over again I think it could have been done less cruelly. The beatings were not necessary; though we thought they were at the time in order to soften them up and stupefy them so that they would die without murmur. It was effective in that sense.

"What a beautiful evening," he said. We looked up. All the constellations were out, amazingly more brilliant than they are over the land. Orion was particularly striking. "However," he continued, "apart from the first few days at Babi Yar, I had little to do with the Jewish problem. I had mostly to do with the gypsies. In Yugoslavia I saw Ustashi militiamen pull children to pieces and beat them to death against trees. The Ustashi were unbelievably savage. On one occasion, I remember, I was ordered to make a girl dig a ditch, while her mother, seven months pregnant, was tied to a tree. I was ordered to open the mother's belly with a knife, take out the baby, and throw it in the ditch. We threw the mother in too, and next the girl, after raping her. We covered them with earth while they were still alive. This is only one example among hundreds, but one of the few occasions when I was ordered to soil my own hands. The gypsies died in a very unseemly way. The Jews were very composed when they went to their deaths – they stood still to be shot; but the gypsies cried, screamed, and moved constantly. After the war was over, I worked in India, Africa, and later in Indo-China.''

"When did you retire?" I asked him.

The old man sighed. "I've never truly retired. One becomes indispensable. Or at least one thinks one does. Actually nobody is indispensable; there is always someone ready to step into your shoes.''

We left it at that, separating to go to our cabins. I saw little of him during the rest of the voyage. Sometimes I caught sight of him, engaging somebody else in earnest conversation, and I guessed he felt a compulsion to go over his story.

Thanks to him, I have an awful night. My fever is back. I am crawling through the desert. In no time, all my cans of cold beer have gone. The ventilation is poor and I can't open the porthole. I can hardly breathe. I try to write a report but I feel too ill. I suppose I do sleep for a while, because I've at last exchanged Zina's house for Olga's. I make for both of us a glass of tea (how bored I am, after twenty years, with plopping into her tea a spoonful of raspberry jam), and sit opposite her, malevolently staring at the gap in her teeth. "Well, this is what you wanted," I snarl. "I didn't," she replies. "I only wanted you to move out of there and live on your own.''

It is unbearable, this heat, this sweat. I go up on deck, wearing only a pair of shorts. There is a clammy mist. I climb up to the boat deck. At first the mist continues to be hot. Standing beneath one of the lifeboats, I think I glimpse the old man. So he can't sleep either. He too has things on his mind. I beat a hasty retreat, having no wish to continue our conversation. And now I am shivering. Not shivering – shaking. I am the Englishman Captain Oates pushing his way into the blizzard. I shake my way back to the cabin, fumble on pyjamas, sweater, socks, and pour myself tea from one of the thermos flasks; but it does not stop me shaking. The cabin is terribly draughty. Gales from the Arctic blow through it. I pile my bunk with blankets and coats, and still I shake. So much shaking makes me hot, and I kick all the coverings off. It is impossible to get cool in this place.

Impossible to sleep. I think I am afraid of falling asleep, so close is sleep to death. I never knew the countries were so close together. I am afraid of the ship going down in the night – and I wouldn't know anything about it.

And now the ship's doctor turns up, with the dawn, and with the Cuban discus-thrower. I don't find her erotic this morning; she threatens me. And indeed, she flips me on to my front, as delicately as a butcher handling a carcass, and jabs a needle into my buttock. She flips me over again. I stare at her angry bulging eyes, her three black chins, the red cross stretched over her enormous white-starched bosom.

She reminds me of Simbi. Simbi rests on a Zimbabwean hillside. I was shown her when I visited the new republic with a delegation of Moscow writers. She has no head and no legs: simply a torso of huge breasts and belly. Every few months the natives come, and fill her with stones and kindling wood. They light the kindling between her thigh stumps, and a great bellows is inserted into her cunt, blowing the fire up. Two men sweat in turns at the bellows; Simbi orgasms in fire, and the bloody iron ore trickles out. The ore is collected in moulds shaped like an infant (and there is an infant shape, too, on Simbi's navel). The ore cools into ingots, the torso goes on orgasming fiercely, men drop from exhaustion and others leap into the breach and pump the bellows. Then at last the natives leave, the fire cools in her belly, and she is left alone with the sacred snake who guards her, coiled on the sacred tree. I stare up at the gross black discus-thrower with hatred.

But the doctor, with his twinkling rimless spectacles, is jovial. He reproves me, though, for writing my journal; I should be resting, sleeping. He suspects I have been sneaking in depression. It is not possible to stop writing, I tell him. He reads the passage I have written about Simbi, and asks me why, if I hate women so, I ever got married in the first place. I say that, on the contrary, I love them. But I fear *their* love a little, because I don't like milk. I married Natalya because, alone of all women, she did not love me. She alone was unimpressed by my poetry. "Your poems bore me, Pushkin," she said once. "You can't imagine," I say, "how sweet that sounded." Natalya wants only to have a good time; to dress up in beautiful clothes, beggaring me, and to go dancing. She hasn't an idea in her head. That too is precious. How delightfully different from these other women with their earnest articulate letters and discussions. Natalya is also beautiful, like the Neva. I can never tire of her. Her sister, Alexandra, is plain, and has a squint. She loves my poetry and loves me. She is also passionate, unlike her sister; and occasionally I sleep with her. "I enjoy screwing her, doctor, but much more I enjoy looking at Natalya."

Shakily I get up and dress, in the afternoon, and sit for a

while on deck. The mist has cleared. The day is bracing. But much too cold. I return to my cabin, and pour myself some hot tea.

It was already dark when Natalya returned from the ball. Removing her cloak quietly, she was obviously trying to undress without disturbing me; but I struggled up from my bunk.

"Was it nice?" I asked her.

"It was all right, Pushkin. But it would have been nicer if you had been able to come."

Poor child, she tries hard to say the right things.

"Yes, I'm sorry too. It's a shame d'Anthès couldn't make it this evening. He could have kept you company." I made the remark lightly and tolerantly, yet with a glint of sharpness, like a razor blade.

She was silent. I heard the crackle of the brush through her beautiful, long light-brown hair. Then she said, equally lightly: "No, he was able to come, actually. He dropped in for an hour."

A current of exhilarated pain ran through me. I lit a cigarette (though it was much less than half an hour since my last), and felt my fingers tremble.

"Did he dance with you?"

"No, of course not! How could you think such a thing?"

I felt relieved and disappointed.

"Why not? You could have danced with him. I trust you."

Still her hairbrush crackled through her hair. "Not after the way he's behaved: never letting me alone; upsetting you; acting in a way that was bound to make people think there was something between us. I made sure I kept my distance."

"He couldn't have liked that very much."

"Oh, he made his usual moon-eyes at me. That tragic, hangdog look."

She started to undress. Her body never ceases to move me. Her breasts were as I imagine Ararat. I caught hold of her hand as she passed, moving towards the wardrobe. "I'm tired, Pushkin," she said.

"Just lie beside me for a few minutes."

She sighed in irritation, but slid under the sheet beside me. I started to have one of my shaking fits, but her flesh brought me no warmth. I kissed her, and her lips, as usual, were cold and unresponsive.

"How many times *did* he kiss you?" I asked. I swallowed involuntarily, knowing she hated to talk about it, but unable to hold back.

"I told you, we hardly even spoke."

"No, I mean – earlier."

"Oh, I don't remember."

"You must have some idea."

She moved her mouth from mine, irritated. "I can't remember stupid details. Why is it important? Not often. Three or four times, I suppose."

"You told me, before, it was only twice."

"Well, it may have been. It depends what you mean by a kiss."

I laid my hand on her right breast. "And how many times did he touch you here?" I swallowed again involuntarily. She did not answer.

She kept her legs closed when I moved my hands between them. Between her thighs she was as cold as a *rusalka*; and she repeated that she was tired. But after a while she let me have my way. I moved inside her, to the creaking movement of the ship. She remained stone-cold, and I was glad.

"You're quite sure he never fucked you?" I said.

She treated the question with scornful silence.

"I can taste him on your lips."

"That's nonsense."

"I have an instinct for knowing. You know that. I'm sure he kissed you tonight."

She says nothing, and I repeat my accusation.

"Why do you keep on at me; what do you want me to say? Yes, all right, he kissed me."

In the surge of jealousy and joy, I so lost control that I almost came. I checked just in time, and all but withdrew from her. "You're only saying that," I said in a voice that shook.

"No, it's true, if you want to know. He danced with me and kissed me."

"A peck, you mean – your cheek?"

"No, my lips. For a long time."

"I hope – I hope you kept your lips closed."

"No, I opened them."

"He kissed you like that in front of everyone?"

"Yes. He doesn't care who knows that he loves me."

"And you didn't care?"

"No, I didn't care."

"Because you love *him*?"

"Yes. Because I love *him*. Madly, if you must know."

I shook with joy. It was the first time I had wrung the truth from her lips. I thrust angrily into her, wanting to tear her apart – the liar! The whore! But she remained calm.

"And you wish *he* were here, fucking you. Don't you?"

"Yes, I wish *he* were here."

"You wouldn't be unresponsive then, would you?"

"No . . . Oh, no!"

"He *has* fucked you, hasn't he?"

"No."

I was angry with her for disappointing me; though I sighed with relief, hearing the note of truth in her voice. She added:

"But he wants to. And I told him tonight that I would, if it weren't for my marriage vows."

I swallowed again, but my throat had hollowed so much I couldn't feel it. "You may," I said. "I want you to. Next time you must say yes."

"All right."

I wrenched myself out, as the seed spilled. After a few moments she fumbled with the sheet and wiped her belly. I held her gently in my arms, covering her hair with kisses. Now that I knew she was lost to me, I loved her more than ever. I loved her because she loved someone else.

There was a quiet knock on the cabin door. "Shit!" I said. I climbed over Natalya and pulled on my dressing-gown. When I opened the door a few inches I saw a sickly yellowish face, on a level with my own. It was Finn. "I'm sorry to bother you in your quarters," he said. "So late too. I fancied a chat."

"I'm sorry," I said, "I've got someone with me. Can it wait?"

He heaved a deep sigh "Yes, of course. It's not important."

But he made no effort to go away.

"It's just," he said quietly, "that I didn't tell you I served in the Ukraine in the early Thirties, during the deportation of the kulaks. And after that I served in Moscow and Leningrad under Yezhov and Beria. They were two very ruthless men. With Beria, I revisited Armenia for a time. There are things I myself sometimes try to forget. I'd like to tell you about that period, sometime. But it doesn't matter now. Perhaps tomorrow, if you can spare an hour?" With yet another sigh, he nodded good night, turned away and walked shakily on his stick along the corridor.

When I closed the door and returned to the bunk, I saw that Natalya had moved across into her own. She said sleepily, "Who was it?"

"A fellow I met yesterday," I said. "He has a lot on his mind."

"Don't we all," she said strangely.

"You should speak for yourself!" But she didn't appear to hear me, having shut her eyes and composed herself to sleep. I sat on her bunk for a while, and felt her little feet under the blanket. They were cold, and I warmed them. She enjoys me rubbing her feet. It's something d'Anthès has never done for her, I dare say. Yet. Her feet are beautiful, so slender and shapely. I hope one day he will have the chance to stroke her feet.

· 2 ·

THE BOOM OF THE SHIP'S FOG-HORN. INSOMNIA. CLAMMY sweat. There is nothing to do but write. I mustn't wake Natalya. Careful not to make too much noise, I fumble in a drawer for my unfinished *Egyptian Nights*; a clean note-book, a pen. I gently kiss her cold brow that dreams of her French guardsman, and slip out of the cabin. I go up to the smoke-room, which is softly lit and empty. Fog curtains the windows. I sit down at a card table, take a cigarette packet and lighter from my dressing-gown pocket and lay them on the table. A small cavity of excitement opens like the crisp white notebook as I start to read the fragment. I rejoice to meet my friends again. How they act and think takes me by surprise.

I grow thirsty, and I interrupt myself to go round the tables collecting undrained glasses. When I sit back down I am surrounded by a good stock of drinks: absinthe, whisky, brandy, gin, beer, vodka, grapefruit juice, benedictine, green chartreuse, advocaat, rum, soda water, vermouth, cointreau. Some glasses have only a few dregs left at the bottom; others have a mouthful or more. There is more than half of a large glass of flat beer.

· (EGYPTIAN NIGHTS, I) ·

Quel est cet homme?
Ha, c'est un bien grand talent, il fait
de sa voix tout ce qu'il veut.
Il devrait bien, madame, s'en faire une
culotte.
THE ALMANAC OF PUNS

Charsky was a native of Petersburg. He was under thirty; he was unmarried; his post in one of the ministries did not weigh heavily upon him. His late uncle, who had been a vice-governor in the good old days, had left him a considerable fortune. His life could have been very pleasant; only he was unfortunate enough to write and publish poems. In journals he was described as a poet, and among servants as a story-teller.

Despite the great privileges enjoyed by poets (though admittedly, apart from the right to use the accusative case in place of the genitive and other similar so-called poetic licences, we know of no especial privileges accorded to Russian poets), despite every possible privilege, these persons are subjected to great disadvantages and unpleasantnesses. The bitterest evil of all and for the poet the most intolerable is the name and title with which he is branded, and from which he can never break away. The public look upon him as their own property; in their opinion, he was born for their *benefit and pleasure*. Should he return from the country, the first person he meets will ask: "Haven't you brought something new back for us?" If his mind is far away, because of his disordered affairs or the illness of someone dear to him, then at once a banal smile will accompany the banal exclamation: "Our friend's composing something!" Is he in love? – then the young woman will buy herself an album at the English shop and expect an elegy. Should he call upon a stranger on some important matters of business, the man will call his small son and make him read aloud so-and-so's verses; and the boy will then treat the poet to the latter's own, mutilated verses. And these are the flowers of his art! What then must be the misfortunes? Charsky confessed that the compliments, the questions, the albums and the small boys irritated him to such an extent that he was constantly forced to restrain himself from making rude remarks.

Charsky made every possible effort to rid himself of the intolerable appellation. He avoided the society of his literary brothers, preferring men of the world, even the most frivolous and empty-headed, to their company. His conversation was extremely commonplace and never touched on literature. In his dress he always observed the prevailing style, with the diffidence and devoutness of a young Muscovite arriving in Petersburg for the first time in his life. In his study, which was furnished like a lady's bedroom, there was nothing to recall the writer: there were no books scattered around, on and under tables; the sofa was not stained with ink; there was none of that disorder which marks the presence of the Muse and the absence of broom and brush. It upset Charsky if any of his worldly friends found him with a pen in hand. He was given to childish pursuits, hard to credit in a man otherwise endowed with talent and soul. At one time he affected to be a passionate lover of horses, at another, a desperate gambler, and at another, a refined gastronome; even though he could not distinguish between horses of mountain and Arab breed, could never remember what was trumps, and secretly preferred a baked potato to all the possible inventions of a French cuisine. He led a life of great distraction; he was to be seen at all the balls, at all the diplomatic dinners, and his presence at a soirée was as inevitable as that of ice creams from Rezanov's.

However, he was a poet, and his passion was insuperable: when he found that his "silly mood" (so did he term his inspiration) was on him, Charsky would shut himself up in his study and write from morning until late at night. He confessed to his genuine friends that it was only then that he knew real happiness. The rest of the time he strolled around, looked official, dissembled, and constantly listened to the famous question: "Haven't you written anything new?"

One morning Charsky felt that happy state of soul when one's imaginings take bodily shape in one's mind, when one finds bright, unexpected words to incarnate the visions, when verses flow easily from one's pen and sonorous rhythms fly to meet harmonious thoughts. Charsky's mind was immersed in sweet oblivion . . . and the world, and the opinions of the world, and his own

personal whims, no longer existed for him. He was
writing verses.

Suddenly the door of his study creaked and an
unfamiliar head showed itself. Charsky gave a start and
frowned.

"Who's there?" he asked irritably, inwardly cursing his
servants who were never in the hall when they should be.

The stranger entered.

He was tall, lean, and seemed to be about thirty. The
features of his swarthy face were expressive: a high, pale
forehead, shaded by dark locks of hair, black sparkling
eyes, an aquiline nose, and a thick beard surrounding
sunken olive cheeks showed him to be a foreigner. He
was wearing a black frock coat, already whitening at the
seams; summer trousers (although the season of autumn
was well advanced); beneath his ragged black cravat,
upon a yellowed shirt front, glittered an artificial
diamond; his shaggy hat seemed to have seen both fine
weather and bad. Meeting such a man in a forest, one
would have taken him for a brigand; in society, for a
political conspirator; in the front hall of someone's house,
for a charlatan trading in elixirs and arsenic.

"What do you want?" Charsky asked him in French.

"Signor," replied the foreigner with a low bow,
"*voglia perdonarmi se . . .*"

Charsky did not offer him a chair; he himself stood up.
The conversation continued in Italian.

"I am a Neapolitan artist," the stranger said, "and
circumstances have forced me to leave my homeland. I
have come to Russia on the strength of my talent."

Charsky imagined that the Neapolitan was intending
to give some concerts on the cello, and was selling his

tickets from door to door. He was on the point of giving
him twenty-five roubles, to get rid of him as quickly as
possible, when the stranger added:

"I hope, Signor, that you will give friendly assistance
to your fellow artist and introduce me to those houses to
which you have access."

It would have been impossible to offer a more painful
affront to Charsky's vanity. He glanced haughtily at this
man who called himself a fellow artist.

"Allow me to ask what sort of a person you are and
whom you take me for?" he asked, with difficulty
restraining his indignation.

The Neapolitan observed his irritation.

"Signor," he answered, stuttering, " . . . *ho creduto* . . .
ho sentito . . . *Sua Eccellenza mi perdonerà* . . ."

"What do you want?" Charsky repeated drily.

"I have heard much of your amazing talent; I am sure
the gentlemen hereabouts account it an honour to accord
every possible protection to so excellent a poet," the
Italian replied; "it is for that reason that I have ventured to
appear before you . . ."

"You are mistaken, Signor," Charsky interrupted
him. "Among us there is no such thing as the calling of a
poet. Our poets have no need of the protection of
gentlemen; our poets are gentlemen themselves, and if
our patrons of literature (devil take them!) are not aware
of this, so much the worse for them. We have no ragged
abbés whom musicians drag off the street to compose
libretti. With us, poets do not go on foot from house to
house begging for help. Moreover, those who told you I
was a great poet were probably joking. It is true, I once
composed a few bad epigrams, but, thank God, I have

nothing in common with our friends the poets, nor do I
wish to."

The poor Italian was confused. He looked around him.
The pictures, the marble statues, the bronzes, the
expensive knick-knacks disposed on Gothic book stands,
struck him. He realized that between the supercilious
dandy who stood before him in a tufted brocade cap, a
gold-embroidered Chinese dressing-gown and a Turkish
sash, and himself, a poor wandering artist, dressed in a
tattered cravat and a threadbare frock coat, there was
nothing in common. He uttered some incoherent
apologies, bowed, and turned to leave. His pathetic
appearance touched Charsky who, for all his faults, had a
kind and generous heart. He felt ashamed of his peevish
vanity.

"Where are you going?" he asked the Italian. "Wait
. . . I felt obliged to disown an undeserved title and
confess that I was not a poet. Now let us talk about your
affairs. I will help you, if it lies within my power. You are
a musician?"

"No, *Eccellenza*," the Italian replied. "I am a poor
improvisatore."

"An *improvisatore*!" exclaimed Charsky, feeling all the
cruelty of the reception he had given. "Why did you not
tell me before that you were an *improvisatore*?" Charsky
grasped the man's hand with a feeling of sincere regret.

Encouraged by this sign of friendliness, the Italian
spoke naïvely of his plans. His outward appearance was
not deceptive: he needed money; somehow in Russia he
hoped to set his personal circumstances to rights.
Charsky listened to him attentively.

"I hope," he said to the poor artist, "that you will have

success. The people of society, here, have never heard an
improvisatore. Their curiosity will be aroused; it is true
that we do not use the Italian language, and you will not
be understood; but that will not greatly matter. The
important thing is for you to create a fashion."

"But if no one understands Italian," said the
improvisatore thoughtfully, "who will come to hear me?"

"They'll come, have no fear: some out of curiosity,
others to pass away an evening somehow, others to show
that they understand Italian. I repeat, the important thing
is that you be in vogue; and you will be in vogue, I
promise you."

Charsky politely dismissed the *improvisatore* after
having taken down his address, and that same evening he
set about trying to help him.

· (II) ·

I am a king, I am a slave,
I am a worm, I am God.
DERZHAVIN

The following day Charsky sought out room number 35
in the dark and dirty corridor of an inn. He stopped at the
door and knocked. The Italian of the previous day
opened the door.

"Victory!" Charsky said to him. "The affair is settled.
The Princess —— offers you her salon. At a big party last
night I succeeded in recruiting half Petersburg. Get your

tickets and programmes printed. I guarantee you, if not a triumph, at least a profit. . . ."

"And that's the main thing!" cried the Italian, expressing his delight by a spate of lively movements, characteristic of his southern origin. "I knew that you would help me. *Corpo di Bacco!* You are a poet like myself, and there's no denying that poets are splendid fellows! How can I express my gratitude? Wait . . . would you like to hear an improvisation?"

"An improvisation! . . . But can you do without an audience, without music, without the thunder of applause?"

"Nonsense! Where could I find a better audience? You are a poet, you will understand me better than others, and your quiet encouragement will mean more to me than whole storms of applause. . . . Find yourself a seat somewhere and give me a theme."

Charsky sat down on a trunk (of the two chairs that stood in that narrow, dingy room, one was broken and the other piled up with papers and underclothes). The *improvisatore* took a guitar from the table and stood before Charsky, plucking at the strings with bony fingers and awaiting his orders.

"Here is your theme," Charsky said to him: "The poet himself should choose the subject of his songs; the crowd has no right to direct his inspiration."

The Italian's eyes glittered, he struck a few chords, proudly raised his head, and passionate verses – the expression of a spontaneous emotion – flew harmoniously from his lips. . . . Here they are, as freely translated by a friend of ours from the words memorized by Charsky:

Eyes open wide, the poet weaves,
Blind as a bat, his urgent way;
But feels a tug upon his sleeve,
And hears a passing stranger say:
"Why do you betray the Muse
By wandering aimlessly, my friend?
Before you reach the heights, you choose
To gaze beneath you, and descend.
Blind to the great harmonious scheme
Of creation, you become possessed,
Too often, by some trivial theme,
And sterile fevers rack your breast.
A genius should look up – the duty
Of a true poet is to rise;
His dwelling place should be the skies;
His theme and inspiration, beauty."
– Why does a wind swirl through a dusty
Ravine and shake its stunted trees,
And yet a ship spread out its thirsty
Canvas in vain for a light breeze?
Why does an eagle leave the peak,
And, gliding past the church spire, seek
The miserable tree stump? Why
Did youthful Desdemona swoon
In the Moor's spasm, as the moon
In the night's shadow loves to lie?
Because for wind, and eagle's claws,
And a girl's heart, there are no laws.
The poet too, like Aquilon,
Lifts what he wants, and bears it on –
Flies like an eagle, heeds no voice
Directing him, spurns all control,

And clasps the idol of his choice,
Like Desdemona, to his soul.

The Italian fell silent. . . . Charsky, astonished and deeply moved, did not speak.

"Well?" asked the *improvisatore*.

Charsky seized his hand and pressed it strongly.

"Well?" asked the *improvisatore*. "What do you think?"

"Astonishing!" the poet replied. "Why, another man's thoughts have scarcely reached your ear before they have become your own, as if you had conceived them, nursed them and developed them over a long period. So, for you there is no toil, no dearth, nor that unrest which is the prelude to inspiration? Astonishing, astonishing!"

The *improvisatore* replied:

"Every talent is beyond explanation. How does a sculptor see, in a block of Carrara marble, the hidden Jupiter, and bring him to light by chipping away with a hammer and chisel? Why does the poet's idea emerge from his head already set in rhyming quatrains and harmoniously scanned? So, none but the *improvisatore* himself can understand that speed of impression, that close link between his own inspiration and a strange external will. . . . I could not even explain it myself. However, we must think of my first night. What do you reckon? What price should I charge for tickets, so as not to overcharge the public and at the same time make sure I don't lose? It's said Signora Catalani took twenty-five roubles a ticket, isn't it? That's a good price. . . ."

It was distasteful to Charsky suddenly to fall from the heights of poetry to the account clerk's desk; but he very well understood the practical necessity of it, and he discussed the financial details with the Italian. The *improvisatore*, in these dealings, demonstrated such savage greed, such an artless love of gain that he revolted Charsky, who made haste to leave him before losing completely that feeling of rapture aroused within him by the brilliant improvisation. The preoccupied Italian did not observe this change of feeling, and he conducted Charsky along the corridor and down the stairs with low bows and assurances of his eternal gratitude.

· (III) ·

The price of a ticket is ten roubles;
the performance begins at seven.
POSTER

The salon of the Princess —— had been placed at the disposal of the *improvisatore*. A dais had been erected and chairs arranged in twelve rows. At seven o'clock on the appointed day, the salon was lit. Selling and collecting tickets at the door, behind a small table, sat a long-nosed old woman wearing a grey hat with broken feathers sticking from it, and with rings on all her fingers. Gendarmes stood near the entrance. The public began to assemble. Charsky was among the first to arrive. He felt largely responsible for the performance, and he wanted to see that the *improvisatore* had everything he needed. He found the Italian in a side room, impatiently looking at his watch. The Italian was theatrically dressed: he was in black from head to foot; the lace collar of his shirt was open, the strange whiteness of his neck contrasted strongly with his thick black beard; his hair had been brushed forward, overshadowing his forehead and eyebrows. All this was not very pleasing to Charsky, who did not like to see a poet in the attire of a travelling magician. After a short conversation he returned to the salon, which was becoming more and more crowded.

Soon all the rows of chairs were occupied by glittering ladies: the gentlemen stood in crowded ranks at either side of the platform, along the walls and behind the last row of chairs. Musicians with their music stands were positioned on both sides of the platform, in the middle of which stood a table bearing a porcelain vase. The audience was large. All impatiently awaited the beginning of the entertainment; at last, at half-past seven, the musicians bestirred themselves, prepared their bows and played the overture to *Tancredi*. There was a settling into seats, and silence; the last strains of the overture rang out. . . . And the *improvisatore*, met by deafening applause which came from every corner of the room, walked forward to the edge of the dais and made a low bow.

Charsky waited uneasily to see what sort of impression the first minute would produce; but he noticed that the theatrical attire, which had seemed to him so unbecoming, did not have the same effect upon the audience. Indeed, Charsky himself found nothing ludicrous in it when he saw the *improvisatore* on stage, his pale face brightly lit by the numerous lamps and candles. The applause died away; the chatter ceased. . . . The Italian, expressing himself in bad French, asked the

gentlemen in his audience to write down some themes for
him on pieces of paper. At this unexpected invitation, all
the men looked at one another in silence. Pausing awhile,
the Italian repeated his request in a timid, humble voice.
Charsky was standing immediately in front of the stage;
he was seized by anxiety; he foresaw that the
performance would not get under way without his help
and that he would be forced to write down some theme.
Indeed, the heads of several ladies turned towards him,
and they began to appeal for his assistance, at first in
whispers, then louder and louder. Hearing Charsky's
name, the *improvisatore* sought him out with his eyes and
discovered him to be standing at his feet; with a friendly
smile he handed him a pencil and piece of paper. To play
a part in this comedy seemed very disagreeable to
Charsky, but there was nothing for it: he took the pencil
and paper from the Italian's hands and scribbled a few
words. The Italian, taking the vase from the table,
stepped down from the platform and held out the vase for
Charsky to drop his theme into it. His example had the
required effect: two journalists, each considering it his
duty as a man of letters to write a subject, did so; the
Secretary of the Neapolitan embassy and a young man
recently returned from a trip spent wandering around
Florence placed their folded pieces of paper in the urn;
finally, with tears in her eyes, a plain young lady wrote at
the insistence of her mother a few lines of Italian and,
blushing to the tips of her ears, handed her piece of paper
to the *improvisatore*, while the other ladies observed her in
silence, with scarcely perceptible smiles. Returning to the
platform, the *improvisatore* put the urn on the table and
began to pick out the pieces of paper one by one, reading

each aloud to the audience:

"La famiglia dei Cenci . . ."

"L'ultimo giorno di Pompei . . ."

"Cleopatra e i suoi amanti . . ."

"La primavera veduta da una prigione . . ."

"Il trionfo di Tasso . . ."

"What is the wish of the honourable audience?" the Italian asked in a humble voice. "Can you agree on one of the proposed themes, or shall we decide it by lot?"

"By lot!" said a voice in the crowd.

"By lot, by lot!" the audience repeated.

The *improvisatore* again stepped down from the dais and, holding the urn in his hands, he asked:

"Who will be so good as to select a subject?" The *improvisatore* cast an imploring glance along the first row of chairs. Not one of the brilliant ladies seated there moved a muscle. The *improvisatore*, unaccustomed to such northern indifference, showed signs of distress. . . . Suddenly he noticed, to one side, a small, white-gloved hand held up; he turned quickly and went towards the dignified and beautiful young lady who was seated at the end of the second row. She stood up, quite unembarrassed, and with the utmost simplicity plunged her aristocratic hand into the vase and drew out a roll of paper.

"Would you be so kind as to unroll it and read it out?" the *improvisatore* said to her. The beautiful young lady unrolled the piece of paper and read aloud:

"Cleopatra e i suoi amanti."

These words were pronounced in a soft voice, but such silence reigned over the salon that they were heard by all. The *improvisatore* bowed low to the young lady, with a look of profound gratitude, and returned to the platform.

"Ladies and gentlemen," he said, turning to his audience, "the lot has indicated as a theme for improvisation: 'Cleopatra and her lovers.' I humbly request the person who chose this subject to explain to me what he had in mind: to which lovers is he referring, *perché la grande regina aveva molto.* . . ."

At these words many of the gentlemen laughed loudly. The *improvisatore* became somewhat confused.

"I should like to know," he continued, "to which historical event the person who has selected this theme alludes. . . . I should be most grateful if he would be good enough to explain."

Nobody hastened to reply. Some of the ladies turned their gaze towards the plain girl who had written a theme at the command of her mother. The poor girl observed this hostile attention and became so confused that tears began to form in her eyes. . . . Charsky could not bear this and, turning to the *improvisatore*, he said to him in Italian:

"The theme was proposed by me. I had in mind a passage of Aurelius Victor's, which suggests that Cleopatra prescribed death as the price of her love. And yet there were found adorers whom such a condition neither frightened nor repelled. . . . It seems to me, however, that the subject is a trifle difficult. . . . Why not choose one of the others?"

But already the *improvisatore* felt the approach of the god. . . . He gave a sign to the musicians to play. . . . His face became terribly pale, he began to tremble as if in the throes of a fever; his eyes glittered with a miraculous fire; he pushed back his black hair, and with a

handkerchief wiped his forehead, which was covered
with beads of sweat. . . . He suddenly stepped forward,
crossed his arms on his chest . . . the music stopped. . . .
The *improvisatore* began.

> The palace gleamed. The sinuous dances
> To flutes and lyres never ceased;
> And the queen's converse and her glances
> Sparkled above the splendid feast;
> All hearts hung on her smile alone,
> But suddenly the queen bowed low,
> Bent forward, smiling, on the throne,
> Touching her goblet with her brow. . . .
>
> The banquet paused as if it slumbered,
> The mirth was hushed, the music checked.
> But now she speaks, no longer cumbered
> By thought, her head once more erect:
> "My royal love you long to savour?
> It is a pleasure you may buy. . . .
> All of my subjects without favour
> I am prepared to satisfy.
> By common lot we'll trade in love.
> The cost, I warn you, is not light.
> Tell me, my princelings, who will give
> His life to share my royal night?
> By the great Mother Goddess, I
> Will serve you in no common fashion;
> Upon the bed of lustful passion
> All of the harlot's wiles I'll ply.
> By the hot Cyprian goddess,
> And by Persephone and Dis

Who twine beneath the earth, I vow
I will exhaust my strong desires
So long as the dark night allow,
And slake you with my secret fires;
Each kiss of mine will bring you joy
That overbrims, yet does not cloy.
But when dawn tints the eastern sky,
Turning black night to purple shade,
All of my happy loves will die
– I swear – beneath the eunuch's blade."

She spoke – and horror seized them all,
And desire trembled in their hearts. . . .
As confused whispers hum, she darts
Impudent scornful eyes along
The ranks of suitors. Suddenly
A man comes shouldering through the throng
Towards the throne, his step firm; he
Is followed by two more; their eyes
Are clear; the monarch rises, greets them.
It's done: three nights, the merchandise;
The bed of love and death awaits them.

Suave priests step forward now and bless
Those three, who plunge their hands into
An urn; the guests sit motionless
And breathless, waiting to see who
Will draw the first night. Flavius
It is – brave warrior, who grew
Grey-headed in the Caesars' pay.
He with the hauteur of a Roman,
Could not endure a scornful woman
Challenging his courage in that way;

For him, no dread lies in her arms
Worse than the battlefield's alarms.
And next is youthful Kriton, born
And nursed in Epicurus' groves,
Kriton who loves, and sings the loves
Of Cupid and the Cyprian. . . .
Attractive to both heart and eyes
Like a spring bud that's not yet blown
Was the third lover. His name lies
In history's chasm. The first down
Was tender on his cheeks; with rapture
His eyes shone; and the untried force
Of passions surged in his young breast. . . .
On him the queen, touched by remorse,
Allowed her proud, sad glance to rest. . . .

I am interrupted by a visitor. She stands before my littered table, a look of relief mixed with annoyance on her pale face. For a few seconds I can't place her at all, this slight figure in a red sweater and gloves, and faded jeans. I am too concerned for Charsky, the *improvisatore*, the nervous young woman with the domineering mother, the cool and elegant beauty who drew out the theme. I wonder what relationship they bear, these women, to Charsky or to the *improvisatore*. I presume they are known to Charsky, but only as faces across a ballroom; or is there a more intimate connection? It is irritating to be interrupted like this, just at the point where inspiration failed before. Perhaps I am fated never to know any more about these people. Flavius, Kriton, and the nameless youth will not enjoy Cleopatra's body, nor suffer the eunuch's blade. Yet I am sure, if this stupid girl hadn't broken in on me, I could have moved their lives forward.

"Why weren't you waiting for me?" she demands. "I've been sitting in your cabin for hours, wondering where you'd got to."

"I'm sorry, Anna," I said – for now I knew who she was, and guiltily remembered that, in an effort to throw her off earlier in the day, I had suggested she might come to me after midnight, if she wanted to. But it wasn't a firm arrangement. "I felt like working," I said, "and the cabin was stuffy."

She sat down opposite, pushed some of the empty glasses away, and rested her head on her arms. "Well, I found you, that's the main thing." Her eyes looked at me brightly, affectionately.

"Yes, you did."

Her unblinking, steady gaze made me uncomfortable. I felt stifled by her presence; couldn't imagine what I'd seen in her that first night. She was far too gaunt; and her fractured Russian, charming at first, had palled. But above all she was too young and inexperienced; an older woman would have sensed that I found her an irritating distraction, and gone away, but Anna was blind to it. I should have been sitting face to face with a different Anna, Anna Kern, mature and elegant like the young lady who had helped the *improvisatore* . . . Anna Petrovna Kern, of whom I had written:

> I remember the moment of wonder:
> You appeared before me,
> Like a momentary vision,
> A spirit of pure beauty.

For years she had resisted me, and then afterwards we had become good friends: which was remarkable. I regretted writing so crudely to a friend that a few days before I had "fucked" Mrs Kern, "with God's help." Such a beautiful, passionate woman, she didn't deserve that senile general as a husband. It was no wonder she had affairs.

Anna Polanski (she is distantly related to the film director) chatters on. Will I take her to see the film *Klute* tomorrow evening? Have I not drunk too much? (I explain that most of the glasses had been almost empty.) Am I not cold? She says it is very cold on deck, and that is why she is wearing her woollen gloves which her grandmother knitted. I listen with half an ear, straining to hear the *improvisatore*, but he has fallen silent. She is speaking now of our "relationship," and I nod absently in the right places.

"I haven't bothered you too much today, have I? I could see you were preoccupied. I didn't mind. I'm glad we talked last night and sorted it out. I don't want to hold you in my pocket – is that the right idiom? I don't mind if we're separated a lot. There are telephones and planes. You don't have to promise to be faithful when you're away from me, though if you make love to anybody I'd rather not know about it. Everything is all right so long as you still love me. You do love me, don't you? You've made me happy. I don't worry at all about the age difference, so it shouldn't bother you either. Do you know this poem by Mickiewicz?" And she quotes a few lines in Polish, and offers me a tender literal translation.

All of this is so boundlessly far from reality, as I see it, that I am perplexed. I cannot believe that I have given her any cause to make these assumptions. I don't recall talking with her last night. She is weaving an adolescent fantasy, but clearly she believes it. This is such elephantiasis of the imagination I can find no words to correct her.

"Look, it fits!" she says, smiling, pulling off a glove, showing me her hand. "I took it to one of the sailors and he was able to tighten it for me." I see the worn gold band with its single poor diamond. I am aghast. It is my mother's engagement ring. I could not possibly have given it to Anna; I would not part with it for the world. Yet she has it, is wearing it, and I presume has not stolen it. In some thoughtless moment last night I must have given it to her.

· 3 ·

IT IS LUCKY THAT ANNA IS A SOLITARY. THOUGH A FEW of the other athletes notice her ring, and congratulate us, I am spared publicity and fuss. She is happy just to be with me. Little by little, from her eager questions, I gather what I must have said to her, in my feverish proposal of marriage. Why, she asks, did I say she looked like the poet Anna Akhmatova, whom I knew when she was old and stout, but loved in her early portraits and photos? (The slender, shapely face, short dark hair, and melancholy smile.) Why was I so sure I loved her, right from our first meeting? (Because she was gentle and unspoiled.) Why did I propose to her while we were actually making love? (Because – and there was truth in this – I had needed to be taken out of myself.) Clasping my hand in her lap, she asks her happy questions as we sit waiting for *Klute* to begin. They have rigged up a screen on the boat deck, since it is a fine, balmy autumn evening.

Her questions sound authentic, not fantasized; and there is that damned ring, pressing against my knuckles. I must have been very ill to have given it up. It is the one keepsake I have of my mother. I came too late to say goodbye; but my daughter Katya, though she was only fifteen at the time, knew enough to slip it from her grandmother's finger. I could put up with the situation with Anna, but for the ring. The voyage would not last forever. A few days and it would be *au revoir*. After a week or so I'd write to say I'd come to realize how unfair it was to burden her with such an age difference. I could express myself fluently in letters, and felt sure I could withdraw with honour. But for the ring. . . . She might refuse to return it. I couldn't take the risk; I had to get it back during the voyage. But I lacked the courage to tell her to her face the engagement was off. I would appear guilty of gross exploitation – and, simply, there was still the ring! She might insist on her rights: that a gift was a gift. She might even tear it from her finger and fling it out through a porthole.

I have seen *Klute* before, at the Writers' Union cinema in Moscow, but it is still entertaining, in its menace. I don't have to talk to Anna, and this is the happiest part of a dreadfully distressing day. Anna, though she knows no English, stares at the screen, where Fonda is under threat from a sex murderer, with a frightened intensity. I glance at her occasionally out of the corner of my eye. She is several years younger than my daughter; it's absurd. I'm intrigued by Fonda – the tough feminist cookie, yet looking so fragile, so vulnerable, in the film, her eyes wide with fright, staring into the sinister darkness of her apartment.

I go with Anna to her cabin, where, with a huge effort

of fantasy displacement, I make love to her. My hands keep hurting themselves against her sharp hip bones and shoulder-blades. She shudders to orgasm; her tenderness turns to drowsiness, and then at last to sleep. When her breathing is slow and deep, I take hold of her finger, and try to ease the ring off. It is too secure; my sly efforts rouse her, and she misinterprets my pulling as a request that we make love again; sleepily, smilingly, she lets her skinny legs fall apart.

I sleep for a few hours. When I wake and get up, and stroll round the deck, the sky and the sea are leaden. Memories, arising from bad dreams, or earlier years with people whom I loved – an unpleasant encounter with Finn – the cold weight of the sea and clouds – oppress me with dreariness. More than dreariness – horror, terror.

Passengers muffled in greatcoats, scarves and hats are being gusted about on the deck. But I swelter, and feel the sweat pouring off me. I gulp ice-cold beer, yet still long to be lying on the iceberg someone has excitedly pointed out, on the horizon.

But the day improves, thanks to a chatty remark thrown out by my anabolic black discus-thrower, when she comes to inject me. I improvise a solution to my problem over the ring. She speaks of her new friend, a Turkish field athlete, who is in despair. She has been offered a scholarship in Texas, but was refused a visa, on the grounds of a (wrongful) conviction for drug-smuggling. She sailed in spite of that, hoping to talk or bribe or screw her way in; but the immigration officer on the ship has confirmed that she will not be admitted.

I tell the black girl I can offer her friend a solution. I happen to hold joint Soviet–American citizenship. My parents emigrated to the New World after the Revolution; but returned in 1930. I was six weeks old when they sailed home. My first memory is of the amniotic flood swirling round me, or the Atlantic Ocean – I'm not sure which. If the Turk and I get married, they'll have to admit her. Once she's in, I tell the black girl, we can go to Reno or Mexico or whatever, and get divorced. I don't need payment, just travelling and hotel expenses.

My black nurse promises to pass on my kind offer to her friend, and in a matter of minutes is back to say that she accepts, gratefully. I am happy to hear that she is not a Moslem – I don't want a wife who covers up everything. There seems no point in delaying the marriage, and I make haste to see the captain and have the whole thing fixed up. There are no complications.

Anna is at first deeply upset, when I tell her; but she realizes it's only a formality and for a week or so. She believes I have made a very Christian gesture. The word makes me smile. I say she is also being very Christian in taking it so well; and I ask for a further sacrifice. It would look odd for her to be wearing my engagement ring when many people will get to know I'm married to the Turk. It might even jeopardize the success of our scheme, for immigration officers are trained to be suspicious. The marriage must appear to be perfectly legitimate. Yes, Anna can see that. She also understands why I'm anxious about the ring's security and want it in my possession. She is loath to give up the token of our love; but she slips it from her finger and gives it to me.

As a thank-offering, I buy her a bottle of perfume at the shop which supplies passengers with everything from tiaras to tampons. There are only three wedding rings left, and I buy the least expensive, asking for a receipt. I can only trust to luck the ring fits.

By cocktail time the wedding party was assembled in the stateroom. Anna was there, and the gross discus-thrower, and Finn, whom I had asked to be my best man. Dressed in a well-tailored pinstripe suit, he played his part with dignity. I had put on my only suit, casual and grey, and a shirt and tie. Anna looked nice in a red dress. The Turkish girl – burly, swarthy, almond-eyed – wore blue dungarees and sandals: smart enough, but not exactly appropriate for a wedding. She thanked me without smiling as we shook hands. I assumed from her dungarees and her sulky expression that she was a feminist. A dungaree'd Turkish feminist, I thought, was perhaps the least conge-nial of all possible brides. It had already struck me as ironic that I, who would be staying in New York with an Armenian American, would arrive there with a Turkish wife. But it did not matter.

It's embarrassing that I don't know her first name. I often miss names on first being introduced; later, it seems stupid to have to ask. I had hoped to learn her name during the ceremony, but it's a difficult name and I still miss it. And when we sign the register her handwriting is as illegible as mine.

I have to get Finn into a quiet corner and whisper: "What's my wife's first name?" "Nayirie," he replies, with a smile and a gust of rancid breath. "It's an ancient royal name among the Armenians."

I am slightly taken aback by the news that my wife is Armenian; but of course I realize there must still be a few Armenians living in Turkey, as there are a few Jews in Germany.

She speaks almost no Russian, and our one attempt at a conversation is a dismal failure. This is at the champagne reception which Finn has very kindly insisted on laying on for us in his suite. While the girls are powdering their noses (though I doubt if Nayirie's nose has ever seen powder) I explain quietly to the old man the nature of this marriage. "You should have told me sooner," he says. "I might have been able to get her in without putting you to all this trouble. I know a few of the right people." He also tells me – and it casts a slight shadow – that I may not find it all that easy to divorce the girl speedily: "Most countries demand a certain minimum duration in a marriage before they will allow it to be dissolved. I speak from bitter experience." I throw off the shadow by drinking lots of champagne, followed by assorted liqueurs.

Suddenly I feel sick and I can hardly breathe in the smoke-filled room – mostly my own smoke, of course. After a few minutes on deck I feel better. I take a few turns round the ship. It feels good to be on my own, breathing the mild, fresh, salty air. The Milky Way is outstanding tonight. The quietness is beautiful. I recall my promise to my doctor not to become involved on this voyage, and start to chuckle; lightly at first, but soon I am cackling: a gust, then a brief pause, then another gust. Yet really, though my situation seems to be more complex, I have simplified it. So, at least, I tell myself.

But when my laughs have exhausted themselves, I lean on the rail and settle into an immense depression. I am here, yet again. The monotonously swirling dark waters are a pattern of my existence. The flecks of foam form themselves into the words of a poem by Blok, which I know by heart. . . .

Night, the street, a lamp, the chemist's:
A dim and apathetic light.
Though you lived on a quarter-century –
Nothing would change. There's no way out.

And if you die – it's but beginning
Over again. All things repeat.
The night. The river's frozen ripple.
The chemist's shop. The lamp. The street.

It would take little for me to clamber over the rail and throw myself into the sea. But if I did, would it be of any use? Would it not happen, just the same, over again? More horrifying still: have I perhaps already died, and are these the dreams of death?

AGAIN I CAN'T SLEEP. I AM BECOMING A PREY TO THE Russian malady. It is that unpredictable missing breath that disturbs me more than anything. But there are also the occasional explosions in my skull, between my ears. This time, even masturbation fails to relax me. The photo that worked the other night – a plump rump in close-up, scored by red suspenders, like the well-fed rump of a French can-can dancer; a hairy, dewy cunt, a man's tongue straining up but for some reason tantalized, not quite able to reach – doesn't stir me enough tonight. Well, it's becoming too familiar. And it's too highly coloured. The English get their porn from Scandinavia, which is almost as boring as the Soviet Union. All that effort of bringing in two magazines (one for the customs official), and for what?

I therefore dress, and go down to the sports room, hoping to find another insomniac who will play me at billiards or snooker. There is no one about, but I decide to knock a few balls around on my own. Even this much exercise, with ash dropping on the cloth, will do me good.

Soon I grow tired of knocking balls around aimlessly. Eventually I hang up the cue and, climbing on to the table, stretch out prone on it. It is something I like to do. I find the closeness of the dazzling green acts on my imagination. And right now I feel a prickling in my nape, and I take a notebook and pencil from my pocket. In exile at Kishinev, which was extremely boring, I wrote *A Prisoner of the Caucasus* while lying like this on a billiard table. Now, for some time, I doodle − sketches of women's faces, bosoms, legs and feet − then an image comes and creates another. I improvise.

· (EGYPTIAN NIGHTS, IV) ·

Give me to drink mandragora. . . .
SHAKESPEARE

The *improvisatore* stopped. He lowered his crossed arms to his sides, and dropped his gaze. He dabbed at his sweat-covered face with his handkerchief. He trembled so violently, and looked so ill, that Charsky was afraid he was going to faint and fall off the rostrum. The Italian quickly composed himself, and took a step back. His own head spinning, from the intensity of his pleasure at the Italian's gift, Charsky glanced around him to see what effect the performance was having on the audience, most of whom, of course, had understood nothing. At that moment the Secretary of the Neapolitan embassy broke

the silence loudly, and this acted as a signal for a whole
storm of applause. One or two of the bolder spirits
among the gentlemen even hazarded "*Bravo!*" The
improvisatore frowned, and raised his arms in an attempt
to quell the noise. He made a gesture towards the
musicians, who immediately started to play a quiet
melody. The clapping died away. The *improvisatore*
closed his eyes. Then, as the audience concentrated again,
he opened his eyes; they glittered feverishly once more.
He pushed back the matted locks of his hair, stepped
forward, and crossed his arms on his chest. . . . The
music stopped. The *improvisatore* continued:

> The queen retires, with her attendants;
> Her eunuch stands outside the doors.
> Tiaras, necklaces and pendants
> Are laid aside; while Iras pours
> Bitter-sweet unguents Sheba used,
> To lave for Solomon her skin,
> Flavius, undaunted but confused,
> Feels, in the dark, the fray begin. . . .
> Touched lightly on his cheek, he quivers,
> He who is scored with livid scars;
> As in his first assault, he shivers,
> Venus controls him now, not Mars.
>
> The night turns silently, the river's
> In flood beneath a million stars;
> The fields are still; the Pyramids
> Are silent as the kings they keep.
> While Mardian sways on guard, his lids
> Heavy, and Iras in her sleep

Entwines with Charmian, the queen
Unrestingly perturbs and charms
The bashful novice in her arms –
A nurse who has to feed, yet wean,
The infant sucking at her breast.
Now teased and pushed away, now pressed
More tightly to her bosom . . . stroked,
Tickled, kissed, hugged, denied, tormented
With hand and tongue and voice, provoked
To pull away, but then prevented,
Held in with all her passion, kept
– It seemed – forever in her womb. . .
The man of iron composure wept.

But quitting Egypt, now, for Rome,
Proud Flavius prepares to die.
The grey-haired soldier is as steady
And dauntless as at Philippi;
Signals to Mardian that he's ready.
The fat impassive eunuch lifts
The monstrous axe; the soul is fled
To where it brings its martial gifts
To lead the cohorts of the dead.

The *improvisatore* paused, but kept his arms crossed on his chest; and this time no applause broke the silence. Charsky, feeling uncomfortably warm in the stuffy salon, mopped his brow, at the same time glancing idly over his shoulder. A sallow-faced lady was staring at him intently. She simpered as she caught his gaze, and Charsky turned his face abruptly to the front. He knew her, only too well, as one of those unhappy women who

pursued him with their vain longings, simply because he
had the reputation of a poet and they had nothing better
to do. The knowledge that her attention had been
directed at him, rather than at the *improvisatore*, irritated
him acutely. But the recital began again, and Charsky
was at once carried in his imagination to the palace in
Egypt.

> Kriton, the scion of love and art,
> Turns from the shadow of desire,
> – Songs he has fashioned for his lyre –
> To plunge into its fiery heart.
> Yet, whether he's too highly strung,
> Or his strength drained away in song,
> He's rigid as the waiting axe:
> Except for one thing, which is lax.
> She understands, and is amused;
> But when an hour's elapsed, confused.
> Perhaps he finds her skin is slack,
> Withered her dugs, her beauty black?
> But no – he only knows the dawn,
> However far away, will break;
> Whether she's gentle as a fawn,
> Or writhes and shudders like a snake,
> He sees her beauty as a swan
> Who sings upon a dying lake.
> In her faint lustrous eyes he senses
> A first reflection of that glow,
> At every silken touch he tenses
> In expectation of the blow.
> It's a gross insult to her pride;
> Her ancestress, the Shulamite,

Was never once unsatisfied;
Nor Cleopatra, till tonight.
Now she is drowsing; she has tried
Everything; it's almost light.

But Kriton lived, as poets must,
Under imagination's sway,
Saw roses spring where all is dust,
And dust where living roses sway.
Now he sees ponderous Mardian loom,
Like a black statue in the gloom.
Perhaps the Cyprian, in compassion,
Bestowed a last gift on her prey,
Granting a swift uprush of passion
To take his fear of death away;
Or, as the night fades, he relaxes,
Could fall asleep, he feels so calm;
The solid appearance of the axe is
A soothing remedy, a balm;
Or seeing Cleopatra, nude,
Her tawny grace, her amplitude:
Who knows what moved him? . . . There's a brief
Explosive burst, a conflagration,
A lightning stroke; then sweet relief
Floods through the queen, and exultation,
Mixed with a little bitter froth,
The knowledge that all beauties fade,
And she will lie, like Sabaoth,
With amorous Kriton in the shade.

The *improvisatore*'s face, hitherto pale, had become
flushed and feverish; his eyes glittered even more wildly;

his shirt was damp with sweat, and the white throat
under his black beard worked spasmodically, as if the lace
collar had been torn open to bare his neck for axe or
guillotine. When he had wiped his forehead dry, the
improvisatore took up his theme.

> Then Cleopatra slept; and woke
> On the third evening, to embrace
> The nameless youth; at midnight's stroke
> She gazed at his enraptured face.
> As in his mouth her tongue takes root,
> They mingle sweat, saliva, breath;
> While nodding Mardian sees a flute
> Call up the swaying serpent, death,
> The boy's slim form, with hers entwining,
> Shows her how quickly he can learn,
> Now coarsening and now refining
> The mutual flame in which they burn.
> Often he gets the upper hand;
> Despite the difference in years,
> She's not completely in command,
> And all distinction disappears.
> Forgetting faithless Antony,
> She is again the tender bride
> Clasped by her brother, Ptolemy,
> Her troth to Caesar cast aside.
> She'd borne then, black as ebony,
> A son, so like him from the start,
> In fear of Caesar's wrath she gave
> Him straightway to a trusted slave,
> Yet ever held him in her heart.
> And this is he — the sable youth

Who loves her, innocent of the truth.
She saw that birthmark on his brow
Before he'd taken his first breath.
Who knows if she's remorseful now
To be the instrument of death?
Maybe her challenge was a whim
When, drunk, she gave no thought to him,
Her youngest squire; or was misled
In thinking him half grown, too young
To be a claimant for her bed,
Since like a desert rose he'd sprung. . . .
Or was she sure the royal line
Had made him passionate and wild,
And threw her challenge by design
To prove her power over her child?
Who knows if, struck by sudden terror
Of slow decline, she wished to see
Her youthful beauty in the mirror
Of yet another Ptolemy? . . .
But there's no doubting the delight
She took of him, until the night
Had all but faded, and the dawn,
Red-lipped as Iras, would soon rest
On her soft couch, and drive her son,
Nephew, and lover, from her breast.

But just before the morning broke,
Before the palace slaves awoke,
He rose, true son of Egypt's star,
Offered the queen cool wine, and threw
In her gold cup mandragora;
Slid a thin dagger from his shoe,

Burst through the doors, slashed Mardian
Who died, amazed, without a sound,
Dashed through the palace, and was gone,
To Asia Minor, and to ground.

As the *improvisatore* spoke the last word, he uncrossed
his arms, bowed abruptly to the audience, and hurried
from the stage. Clamorous applause brought him back;
he bowed again, from the waist, his black hair flopping.
The rapturous clapping continued; and between bows
and courteous gestures towards the musicians, he broke
into a delighted smile, his teeth brightly gleaming above
the black beard. With a final profound bow he left the
rostrum again; the clapping died away; a buzz of
conversation ensued, and those who were near the doors
began to drift through, to where refreshments were to be
served during the interval.

· (V) ·

*I have married a wife, and therefore I
cannot come.*
ST. LUKE'S GOSPEL

Standing in the Princess —— 's reception room,
surrounded by loudly talking people sipping tea from
green cups and nibbling at sweetmeats, Charsky was
assailed at every hand by congratulations. "I am nothing
but the go-between," he protested; "but all the same, I
agree with you that it is an extraordinary gift."

"So extraordinary," said the sallow lady who had stared at the back of Charsky's head throughout the performance, "that I suspect you have been up to something! Confess it, you arranged for your theme to be chosen, and your Italian friend prepared it beforehand! Indeed, perhaps you wrote it yourself, and only gave it to him to memorize! You are playing a joke on us!" With an accusing simper, she rolled her faded eyes at him. Charsky stared down at her, frowning. Knowing that she was only attempting to attract his attention, but finding this just as offensive as a serious accusation of deceit, he replied frigidly: "If you had the least understanding of those verses, you would know I could not possibly have composed them."

Her eyes filled with alarm, her scrawny bosom heaved, her reedy voice quivered as though Charsky was threatening to strike her. "I was not serious, Charsky," she said, in a plaintive and querulous tone.

"I'm glad to hear that." He added, a shade more gently: "There is no trick, I can assure you."

"Then it must be a miracle," said a soft voice from somewhere behind him. Turning, he found himself looking into the eyes of the plain young lady who had written a theme at the insistence of her mother. Charsky smiled, and the young woman blushed and dropped her gaze, murmuring, "I'm sorry, it was rude of me to break in."

"Not at all. I wished to thank you for so kindly helping to get the performance started. But whom have I the pleasure of thanking?"

"Katerina Orlov. But really, it is I who should be thanking you, for this unforgettable evening."

Charsky gave the plain young woman all his attention, and with his turned back dismissed the foolish, besotted lady. "You think it is a miracle? Well, yes, it is, in a way. I don't understand it any more than I understand why that gentleman over there has orange hair. . . ." He nodded in the direction of an elderly fop, Count O——, who was conversing with the bedraggled and eccentric old woman who had sold tickets. "He has just congratulated me on the wonderful poetry," Charsky continued pleasantly, "though he knows no Italian, and indeed scarcely knows French. Russian is as closed a book to him as Italian, of course. He is, as you probably know, one of our leading literary censors, and certainly the most reasonable. It's all miraculous, don't you think?"

The poor girl was silent, and her cheeks remained flushed. Charsky, realizing that she probably thought he was teasing her, quickly brought himself back to the evening's performance, by enquiring if she had found it entertaining. Her mild eyes lit up. "Oh, it is wonderful!"

"You are one of the very few people present who understood the *improvisatore*'s verses. Tell me what you truly thought of 'Cleopatra e i suoi amanti.' I trust you weren't offended by it?"

Two flames burned again on her cheeks, and she bent her head. Then, lifting her gaze, she said: "Is it possible anyone could have been offended?"

"It is possible," he said drily.

"No, I was not offended. The theme demanded it. . . . A wonderful theme," she added hastily.

"I should like to know which theme you yourself wrote down, but it would be rude of me to enquire."

The plain young woman gave a slight smile. "Not at all. '*La famiglia dei Cenci.*'"

"That was a well-chosen theme." Charsky was glancing round the crowded room, trying to catch a glimpse of the elegant young lady who had drawn out the theme for improvisation; she was a stranger to him, and had aroused his interest. Failing to catch sight of her in the throng, he went on: "How do you come to know Italian?"

Charsky's attention still wandered from time to time as the young woman told him that she had fallen ill, and her mother had taken her to Italy in the hope that the warm climate would cure her. She had picked up a certain amount of Italian, but not nearly so much as her mother fondly believed. They were on their way home to Moscow, having visited Germany *en route*, but were resting for a few days with relations in Petersburg. They would be leaving tomorrow.

"And I trust your health is better?" he asked gently, understanding now why the flames sprang so readily to her pale face.

While she hesitated, a footman announced in a loud voice that the performance was ready to begin again. The ladies and gentlemen began to drift towards the doors. The young woman's mother came up to rejoin her, and Charsky slipped away.

When the salon was full, and the *improvisatore* had returned to the stage and acknowledged the applause, he asked the audience if they wished to go on choosing themes by lot from the original list, or to write down some new ones. Charsky, guessing that he would prefer a fresh list, asked him in a clear voice to confirm that it would be acceptable to write down the themes in French. The *improvisatore* agreed; at this, the audience clamoured for a new list to be prepared, and very many of them indicated their willingness to take part. Once more the Neapolitan asked the elegant young lady to help; graciously she nodded. He asked her to draw out three pieces of paper from the score or so that had been dropped in the vase. He would attempt all three, in quick succession. The young lady, who was wearing a simple lilac-coloured dress and white gloves, drew out three papers, unrolled them, and announced the first and the second themes; when she came to the third, a ripple of amusement ran round the audience, for she had read out: "'The beauty in the lilac dress.'" With a barely perceptible smile, looking in no way embarrassed, she dropped the paper back into the vase.

Charsky, who had not, in fact, been responsible for the theme of Cleopatra, but had only stepped in because no one would admit to it and a young woman was being distressed, was amused and pleased to find that this time his theme had actually been chosen. The simplicity of the *improvisatore*'s helper moved him. He wondered where such a beauty could have been hiding in St Petersburg. At the end of the performance he determined to intercept her before she could leave, with the excuse of thanking her for her contribution. While the Italian declaimed, Charsky kept glancing discreetly at her. Her gaze never wavered from the *improvisatore*. Charsky lost many of the verses in the golden coils of her hair, her full lips, her voluptuous figure, her lustrous eyes.

It is true, he thought, that her face is somewhat fleshy; indeed, she has the beginnings of a double chin; yet everything is so harmonious that even that defect is a grace.

To his disappointment, the Italian's improvised verses on "The beauty in the lilac dress" failed to do her justice; they were competent, but lacking in inspiration, compared with his earlier efforts. He did not even glance in her direction. He was growing tired, Charsky thought; and so was the audience, wearying of an unintelligible language and eager for more frivolous pursuits. There was relief as well as genuine appreciation in the loud clapping and *Bravos!* which brought the pale, sweating *improvisatore* back to the platform several times.

Charsky had pushed his way to the back and was standing by the doors almost before anyone had left; yet, when the last few people were making their way out, he realized he had missed the beautiful young lady. He had to make do with talking to the long-nosed old woman who chattered to him volubly as she counted the takings. The orange-haired government censor glided up to join them. When the fop renewed his effusive congratulations, Charsky responded amiably, for, in spite of everything, he respected the Count as a decent individual whose "heart was in the right place."

Disconsolate at the disappearance of the unknown beauty, Charsky forced himself to think of the grand success of the evening. He was delighted for the *improvisatore*'s sake; and started also to anticipate the pleasure of a good dinner, and the marvellous gypsy dancer with whom he was on close terms, and the prospect of a game of cards. Charsky could not be despondent for long.

The *improvisatore* was slumped, white-faced, in a chair

in the side room. He, too, cheered up and grew animated when Charsky showed him the plateful of roubles. Leaping to his feet, he seized the plate from Charsky's hands.

"*Meraviglioso! Quanto denaro c'è,* Signor?"

"Enough to enable you to leave that filthy inn," said Charsky, "and move into the Demuth. Pack your trunk, pay your bill, and I'll send a coach tomorrow to take you there."

An expression of distress came over the Italian's face. He stammered that he was quite happy at the inn; it was inexpensive, and he wished to live as cheaply as possible. Charsky shrugged, and then invited him out to dinner. The Italian, evidently not realizing that Charsky intended to pay, looked even more disturbed, and said he was not hungry. When Charsky explained that he wished to show his appreciation of a wonderful performance, the Italian accepted eagerly.

On their way to the restaurant, Charsky tried to engage the Italian in conversation about the creative inspiration which had so filled his sails that evening; but the *improvisatore,* ignoring these overtures, insisted on discussing with him how best to obtain further engagements.

"They will come," said Charsky, "have no fear. The word will spread like wildfire, and soon it will be a disgrace not to have heard you."

"Then do you think we should charge more next time? Or would we be in danger of killing the goose that lays the golden egg? What do you think, *Eccellenza*? . . ."

So the conversation continued, both in the coach and while they were waiting for their beefsteak to be served.

Then the Italian bent over his plate as greedily as he had bent over the plate of roubles. He did not appear to notice the gypsy band, nor the lithe gypsy dancer who performed near their table, responsive to Charsky's sparkling eyes.

When the *improvisatore* finally sank back with a sigh of contentment, he said to Charsky, "Pardon me, Signor . . . but I would like to ask you another favour. If you could only find a translator for one or other of my poor improvisations, and have it published in one of your excellent periodicals, that would make me better known, don't you think?"

Charsky warmed to the suggestion at once.

"Which improvisation do you suggest?" he enquired.

"Which do you think, Signor? '*Cleopatra e i suoi amanti?*' I think that was my best."

"You're probably right. The love of power giving way to the power of love. Wonderful! Either that one or 'Jupiter and Ganymede.'"

The Neapolitan frowned. "I was less happy with that one. It was not a subject which inspired me."

"Very well. The 'Cleopatra' was an astonishing improvisation. I will gladly attempt to translate it myself, if you will permit. I am fairly sure the editor of *The Contemporary* – himself a splendid poet who would certainly have come to hear you tonight if he were not preoccupied with domestic quarrels and the malice of the Court – will take it. I refer to Pushkin. Of course I shall have to tone it down, to satisfy our blue-nosed censors."

"*Eccellenza*, you do me too great honour!" exclaimed the *improvisatore* joyfully. "I will write it down for you this very evening."

Charsky, who prided himself on his excellent
memory, said there was no need.

"How much does this journal you mention pay per
line?" asked the Italian eagerly. Detecting a note of
irritation in Charsky's reply, he hastened to explain that
he needed all the money he could get. "My affairs are in a
bad way, and I have a family to support: *mia moglie e i miei
cinque bambini*. . . ." A tender look came over his face as
he uttered those words.

He produced from an inside pocket a tiny album,
which he handed to Charsky. The yellow pages of the
little book were filled with delicate sketches of a woman's
face. The face reminded Charsky of the heavy pudding
which they had just eaten. "*Mia moglie*," explained the
Italian reverently, and his eyes glistened with tears. There
were sketches, also, of children, ranging in age from
earliest infancy to seven or eight.

"You have a charming family," observed Charsky,
"and your concern for them does you credit. But tonight
you are in Petersburg, and we are going to celebrate your
success! What do you say to a game of cards with some
friends of mine, followed by a visit to a house where the
girls, I can promise you, are even more splendid than
your famed Neapolitan beauties?"

The Italian, with a look of horror, stammered his
apologies. "*Eccellenza, non capisco . . . Sua Eccellenza mi
perdonerà, ma . . .* You forget, I am married. . . . You
have seen my wife, and I assure you she is even lovelier
than in my poor sketches. . . . It would be impossible for
me to betray such a woman."

· (VI) ·

*For sale, girl of sixteen, excellent
conduct, and a barouche, in fair condition.*
ADVERTISEMENT

Charsky had been driven back to his house when the
dawn was breaking and the streets were empty except for
artisans trudging to their work. He went to bed and woke
up at his customary time, about three in the afternoon.
He tugged on the bell rope, and his valet appeared with
tea and the day's letters on a silver tray. Charsky sipped
the tea and slit open his mail. One of the letters agitated
him so much that he had to get up, put on his
dressing-gown, and pace round the room. He tugged on
the rope again, and ordered his startled man to prepare at
once to set out for Moscow.

He found himself sharing the coach journey with
Madame Orlov and her daughter. They were greatly
surprised to see him. "You see," he said to them with a
smile, "we try to be well-mannered in Petersburg. . . . I
did not like to think of you travelling alone!"

But at the first staging post, while they drank poor
coffee before a low fire, he explained the reason for his
unexpected journey. "I received a letter," he said, "from
a close friend of mine, to say that he is getting married.
It's an absurd match, and I must try to prevent it. I only
hope I'm not too late. He's young and impetuous. He
already has a lovely wife, in Petersburg; or rather, he did.
He's actually divorced her for being unfaithful!"

"And has she been?" asked Katerina.

"She has had flirtations. Nothing to threaten their marriage. Besides, my friend encouraged her in these since he himself enjoyed his freedom. His wife put up with a great deal. So did I, as a matter of fact; I've often had to get my friend out of trouble. You'll never believe what happened, but I assure you it's true. He decided he needed a new carriage, and saw one advertised very cheap, along with a servant girl. The carriage was a bad bargain – its springs soon went . . . but he fell in love with the girl! He threw up everything, resigned his commission, and went to Moscow with her. He decided she has a talent for acting, and found a friend in Moscow, a director, who is willing to try her out. My friend is besotted with her. I hoped it would blow over quickly, but now he is actually planning to marry her!"

During the tedious and uncomfortable journey, Charsky was very concerned for the well-being of the young woman. It was clear that her visit to Italy had by no means cured her of her consumption. He did his best, over the three days, to cheer her up and take her mind off her suffering by talking to her about the wonders she had seen in Italy. He found her a pleasant travelling companion: intelligent, quiet, and free of self-pity. He promised to call on her, after she had had a week or so to recover her health, and take her out for a drive. She expressed a touching gratitude for his kindness; to which Charsky replied, with genuine warmth, that it was not kindness: the pleasure would be all his.

Arriving in Moscow on an afternoon of cold autumn drizzle, Charsky settled into a comfortable hotel, changed his clothes, and set out without delay to call on his friend. The grimy street corresponding to the address on Kornilov's letters confirmed him in his forebodings.

He was greeted not by a footman but by Kornilov himself, in dressing-gown and slippers. He looked as if he had not washed or shaved for two days; there were dark circles round his eyes. He swayed drunkenly as he contemplated his visitor.

"Why, Charsky! How delightful!"

"Am I too late?" Charsky demanded.

"For the ceremony? . . . Yes, we're married. . . . I had to strike while the iron was hot! It was a devil of a job persuading her to take me on! But you're here for the celebration – that's grand! Natasha will be thrilled! Come inside: there are lots of old friends here. . . ."

He took Charsky by the arm and led him into a gloomy room (though it was still daylight, the curtains were drawn), and at first Charsky could make out nothing except some vague shapes strewn around on the floor. He found it hard to breathe in the sweet, heavy atmosphere. "It's Charsky!" Kornilov announced in a booming, dignified tone. Some of the vague shapes slowly got to their feet, and Charsky recognized Muscovite acquaintances. Surrounding him, they mumbled drunken greetings, and pawed his clothes in a way he found distasteful. Then the shape of a female pushed her way through and flung her arms round his neck. "Charsky!" she cried. "Why didn't you come in time for our wedding?"

Natasha was also still in a dressing-gown, and her hair was disarranged. Charsky withdrew from her embrace, and the young woman put her arms round Kornilov's neck. The newly-weds swayed around in each other's arms, giggling, covering one another's face with kisses.

"Where are you staying?" asked Natasha, disengaging at last from her bridegroom. "He must move in with us, mustn't he, Ivan?"

"If you don't mind the mess, Charsky. You might be more comfortable at the hotel. But of course you're welcome to stay with us; you know that."

Charsky, who had indeed anticipated that he would probably move out of the hotel to stay with his friend for a few days, was glad to seize an excuse not to do so. He did not wish to crowd them, at this time; and besides, he needed to do some work. In fact, he could not stay even now; he must settle in. Kornilov nodded amiably, and thrust a glass into his hand. Charsky allowed the glass to be filled. "I drink to your happiness," he said; but refused a second, saying that he must really be off. Kornilov stumbled outside with him. "Join us later, won't you? We're all going to the theatre. Natasha has her first part. She's really wonderfully talented! Do come; she's made me so happy." He added, in a voice which trembled: "She's my last chance of happiness."

Charsky gazed straight into his friend's eyes, shook his head with a sigh, and turned away.

The play in which Kornilov's bride was performing, in an unfashionable theatre, bored Charsky unutterably; and Natasha seemed to him as wooden on stage as she was dramatic in real life. Yet Kornilov, sitting beside him, devoured her performance avidly, and Charsky could feel his body tremble as the plot called for her to be embraced by the hero. And afterwards he caused a scene in a restaurant when the same individual paid her what her husband considered to be too much attention. She flared up in return when Kornilov said something in a low voice to the pretty wife of one of his acquaintances. Natasha made a remark which the whole company could hear; Kornilov responded coarsely; yet the next moment they were fondling each other in full view of everyone, and laughing like children.

The following day Charsky dined alone with them at their house; but found the atmosphere so stifling that he resolved not to go again. He smelt disaster in the over-intense emotion of the ill-matched couple. It's like coupling with Cleopatra, every moment of the day, every day of the year, Charsky thought to himself, when he had regained the freedom of his spacious hotel room. Reminded by this thought of his promise to the *improvisatore*, Charsky straightaway set about recalling the Italian strophes, and in the space of an hour or two dashed off a translation. He read it through with satisfaction, altering a word here and there. Then he scrawled a note to Pushkin; placed it, with the translation, in an envelope which he sealed and addressed; and rang the bell summoning a servant.

To his surprise the landlord himself knocked on his door and entered, took the letter, and announced that a young lady had called to see him. Charsky, curious, wondering if this was to be some strange amorous adventure, told the man to bring her up. Natasha Kornilov appeared. She excused herself for having disturbed him so soon after he had left them; but she happened to be on her way to the theatre, and she was calling on the spur of the moment to ask his advice. Simply, she wondered how she could cope with her husband. He was so melancholy, much of the time, so dark in his moods, so disordered in his habits. Charsky

advised her not to keep him on too tight a rein; but
Natasha protested it was quite the reverse: Kornilov
clung on to *her*. Charsky sighed, and said, "Yes, I'm sure
that's true."

They talked for about half an hour. Charsky found her
much more pleasant and unaffected away from Kornilov,
and warmed to her. She was of course terribly immature;
but that was to be expected in a girl of eighteen, a freed
serf, badly educated. He believed her now to be sincere in
her desire to make her husband happy. He even found a
certain charm in her small plump body, her coarse
features, her wiry black hair, and the rather acrid scent
clinging to her. She had an animal vitality; but for how
long would she keep it, married to Kornilov?

He kissed her hand from an unexpected impulse of
tenderness as she took her leave.

Charsky was as good as his word in calling on Katerina
Orlov. When the first snows of the winter had fallen, he
took her out for a sleigh ride. Snug under furs and
blankets they bowled along, by the river shod with ice
and out into the forests. The wind whipped through
them and howled, but her thin face glowed.

Postponing his return to Petersburg from day to day,
and week to week, he called for her almost every
afternoon. Sometimes she felt too ill to go out; too ill
even to leave her divan. On these occasions Charsky sat
with her; they would chat and read together, and
Madame Orlov would bring them tea. Once, he bent
swiftly over Katerina's plain, wan face and pressed his
lips to hers. . . .

He confessed to Kornilov, on a rare evening when they
were drinking alone together as in the old days, that the

danger of her mother's bursting in on them was an attraction. As indeed was the young woman's serious illness: the unnatural glitter in her cheeks and eyes, the transparency of her skin, the almost vanished colour of her lips. Charsky was aware of a morbid fascination with the fact that she was alive, and vibrant, panting, her face flushed, her hair awry . . . but for how much longer?

"Why should this be?" he asked the younger man. "Can you explain it? Have you ever been in love with a consumptive?"

Kornilov responded quite in the old, pleasantly cynical manner. But he had changed nonetheless, Charsky observed. He spoke and listened from somewhere above the fray. His swarthy face was growing sleek. His air of the "settled married man" vexed Charsky, who started to try to find some chink in his armour. He casually brought his friend's former wife into the conversation: spoke of visiting her in the large, elegant house which Kornilov affected not to miss. He mentioned having glimpsed his friend's favourite wolfhound.

He noticed that Kornilov's eyes had grown moist. The sight astonished him. He had seen him often enough sunk in melancholy; but usually he covered those moods with boisterous humour, or dramatized them with dark rages, outbursts against women or against religion. Alternatively, he got drunk and passed out. But Charsky had never seen him weep. It quite unnerved him, and he stammered some sort of apology, which his friend, wiping his eyes with one finger, waved away with his other hand.

· (VII) ·

Dans l'adversité de nos meilleurs amis,
nous trouvons quelquechose qui ne nous
déplaît pas.

LA ROCHEFOUCAULD

One wintry night, when Charsky had returned from an evening at the Orlovs', he found waiting for him a note that had been delivered by a groom. The note was from Kornilov, in a shaky hand bidding him farewell; thanking him for all he had done to help him; saying it had been an honour to have known him; asking him to do his best for both "Natasha and my wife." He was, he wrote, going to "a quiet region" to which he felt he truly belonged. After reading the note three or four times, Charsky felt a prickling at his nape, and was convinced that his friend had blown his brains out. Immediately he ordered his groom to harness up the horses again; and drove off into the blizzard towards his friend's house.

As the sledge whirled through the densely falling snow he felt his nerves strung up unbearably tight. Already he felt stricken by grief; yet at the same time excited by such a dramatic event at the end of a pleasant, but rather tame, evening with Katerina and her mother. Natasha would be there, weeping inconsolably, and he wondered what he could say to her. It would fall to him to inform Kornilov's parents, and his former wife, who would also be distraught.

However, when they reached the dingy house, he found his friend, in good health, supervising the packing of a trunk. Kornilov was surprised, and clearly put out, by Charsky's arrival. He had hoped, he explained, to get away without the tedium of goodbyes. Natasha was away staying with friends; she would find a letter for her on her return: if indeed she ever returned. Their situation had grown increasingly intolerable. He was releasing her from the nightmare into which he had dragged her. He planned to go south to Erzerum in Armenia, on the borders of the Empire. He had visited it once before, while serving with the army, and found it tranquil.

Charsky, knowing it would be pointless to argue, embraced him in brotherly fashion, wished him good luck, and quietly left. As Kornilov yielded to his urge to go somewhere far away, Charsky simultaneously found his thoughts turning towards home. A few days later, after a more prolonged and uncomfortable leave-taking at the Orlovs', he left Moscow for his native city.

Upon his arrival in Petersburg, Charsky went straight to his study, without taking off his overcoat, hat and gloves; and after warming himself at the fire he sat down at his desk and started to skim through various letters which the servants had neglected to send on, or which had arrived only in the past few days. He glanced around his room with quiet pleasure: the portraits and landscapes, the marble statues and the bronzes, the Gothic book stands . . . all were as he remembered. He rang the bell for his valet, who helped him to remove his wet outer garments. He ordered champagne.

Over Veuve Cliquot, he cut the fresh-smelling leaves of *The Contemporary*, and found "Cleopatra and her Lovers." Pushkin had been as good as his word in finding a space in the current issue: that was decent of him. It was also surprising and gratifying that the censors had not insisted on any cuts or changes.

The champagne, after the long, tedious journey, relaxed him and made him feel sleepy. He was actually drowsing off in his chair when a noise startled him and he awoke with a jump. A man was standing by the open door; it was the *improvisatore*. Despite the freezing weather outside, he wore the same black frock coat, looking still more frayed and faded, as he had worn on his first visit in autumn. His hair and beard were covered in snow.

Charsky said, without rising: "How nice of you to call! Who told you I was back? Are you well?"

"I have a cold, *Eccellenza*." The Italian's teeth were chattering and he was shaking all over.

"I'm sorry to hear that. You're not used to our Petersburg winters. Come and warm yourself, and have some champagne. . . . Or would you prefer something hot? No? Well, tell me your news. Have you made lots of money? I hear you performed before the Tsar? . . ."

"Yes, *Eccellenza*."

"Splendid. But really, you're perishing! Draw up a chair to the fire. Have you read this? I've only just seen it myself. What do you think of my translation? I hope you don't think it's too free? . . ."

"Signor," interrupted the Italian urgently, "I am in great need of your help."

"I shall be only too pleased. As you can see, I have only this minute returned, but . . ."

"It won't wait, Signor. Read this, please." He took out from his inside pocket a crumpled letter, and handed it to Charsky. Charsky read it and stood up, frowning.

"It is a challenge to a duel," he observed. "This gentleman thinks you have insulted him. What have you been up to?"

"Nothing," said the Neapolitan, his teeth chattering in his skull even more violently than before. "I have never heard of him. *Non capisco.* I do not understand. How can I have insulted someone I do not even know, have never seen?"

"This Count O—— is a bit of an idiot, but his heart is in the right place. He was at your first performance. You must have caught sight of him – at that time at least, he had dyed his hair orange; you could hardly have missed him."

"I am colour-blind, Signor."

"Are you, by Jove? Why, that explains it! You could not have known who was wearing a lilac dress! . . . Well, anyway, I'll call on the Count. This very day: I'm sure we'll find it's a misunderstanding. Leave it to me. Go back to your inn now and wait for me to come. Don't worry, I'll clear up the mystery."

The Italian broke into a relieved smile, and left with profuse expressions of gratitude.

· (VIII) ·

He was within a few hours of giving his enemies the slip forever.
STERNE

The *improvisatore*'s room, so far as Charsky could judge by the light of a feeble candle, for darkness had fallen, had changed little since his previous visit. One chair was still piled high with papers and linen; the other had not been repaired or replaced. The only novelty was a picture of the Virgin, behind cracked glass, over the bed. The *improvisatore* was lying on the bed when Charsky entered: a blanket pulled around him. Icicles hung from the top of the curtainless window.

Retaining his coat, but pulling off his frost-rimmed fur hat and resting it on his knees, Charsky announced to the shivering *improvisatore* that it was all the fault of his wretched translation. With difficulty he suppressed a joyous smile, because the story he had to tell was so droll, but he managed to keep his face grave, in tune with the Italian's anxiety and the genuine seriousness of the situation.

"The Count thinks your verses are making a laughing-stock of him," said Charsky. "He thinks they were a thinly disguised portrayal of his family circumstances. In short, that your Cleopatra is his mother!

"She was the old madam with the long nose and the broken feather who very kindly agreed to sell tickets at the door for your first performance. She used to bear the nickname of 'Cleopatra': presumably because she was beautiful (though it's hard to credit now), dissolute to an extreme – even by Petersburg standards – and had a long nose. Her beauty has faded, her dissoluteness finds no takers, but her nose remains. In her youth and middle years she was the mistress of a soldier and a poet, Kutuzov and Derzhavin. This is well known. She is said to have killed them both off with the strenuousness of her demands. Napoleon didn't wreck Kutuzov's health – she

did. Or so they say. You begin to see the resemblance to
'*Cleopatra e i suoi amanti*'?"

"*Dio mio!*" groaned the Italian. "*E assurdo!*"

"You are right. But the coincidence doesn't end there.
She is said to have taken her own brother, a notable rake,
into her bed; furthermore it's rumoured that Count
O—— is their offspring. I have even heard it suggested
that the son himself was, at one time, not immune to her
lust. Of course, the Count didn't bring up these aspects of
his mother's fame; only Kutuzov and Derzhavin. But I
could read his thoughts. A stale scandal, an almost
forgotten legend, is painted in glowing colours in the
pages of our leading progressive journal. . . ."

"*Non capisco*, Signor," moaned the poor Italian, sitting
up straight in the bed and burying his head in his hands.

"It's really an amazing coincidence," Charsky
continued remorselessly. "I'm astonished that it didn't
strike me at the time. But I was too overcome by the
splendour of your gift. Of course, the Count is neither
young nor black-skinned, but he does have a birthmark
on his forehead. . . ."

The Italian took his hands from his face and exclaimed
agitatedly: "*Ma come potevo saperlo*? . . . How does he
imagine I knew about this? *Come sa che conosco i suoi
affari*? . . . I was not even sure what the theme demanded,
until you explained to me."

"It so happens he knows I wasn't the author of the
theme. I spoke of it in passing when we chatted during
the interval of your performance. He believes the true
author was the Secretary of the Neapolitan embassy, a
personal enemy of his. Some matter of an IOU the Count

is accused of not honouring. . . . Not unlike your third lover who did not honour his agreement. He has discovered that the young lady who drew out the themes was a niece of the Neapolitan diplomat, on a visit to her uncle. . . ."

The *improvisatore* was rocking backward and forward in his distress, and moaning softly to himself. The moan was cut short by a loud sneeze.

"The Count believes you may have called at your embassy on arrival. . . . Did you, as a matter of fact?"

"*Certo, ma* . . ."

"And the Secretary cooked up a scheme to make a fool of him. You were bribed into preparing those verses, and also told to seek me out and ask for my help, since I have the ear of the liberal press who could be counted on to publish a translation of such an exotic and indecorous work. Probably the Court knows about it and winked at it. They would not turn away from the chance to harm Count O——, who is the nearest to a friend we have among the literary censors, while at the same time – in the guise of righteous indignation on his behalf – finding an excuse to attack us so-called liberals. . . . Those few of us who are not rotting in Siberia. . . Now do you understand the reason behind the Count's challenge?"

The *improvisatore* sneezed again, and followed this with a moan. "So you too have turned against me, *Eccellenza*!"

Changing his tone completely, Charsky said: "Of course not, my friend! The Count is angry and upset, and therefore has conjured an absurd theory out of thin air. I know you respect your art too much to cheat the public. Besides, unlike the Count, I have had the advantage of hearing your astonishing gift at first hand, when there could have been no possibility of a trick. The Count has been misled by his irascible nature, weak intellect, and the normal coincidences that attend the creation of any work of art. But I could not persuade him that he is mistaken. The best I could do was to make him admit that you probably were led astray only out of a desire to provide for your family. He will therefore be content with a written apology. So you can cheer up! All is well!''

"I cannot apologize, Signor. This Count has insulted my honour.''

"Then you will have to fight him,'' Charsky warned, smiling to himself at the absurd picture the idea conjured up.

The *improvisatore* shrugged his shoulders.

"How are you at handling a pistol?''

"I have never handled one, *Eccellenza*.''

"In that case, my dear fellow, you must swallow your pride. The Count is a crack shot despite his age. He insists on a duel or an apology within twenty-four hours.''

The Italian repeated that it was impossible for him to apologize for an offence he had not committed.

"Then tomorrow your wife will be a widow and your five *bambini* will be fatherless.''

Seeing the Italian look a trifle disconcerted, Charsky pressed the point home: "That means, tomorrow before sunset, at latest.''

"Very well,'' said the *improvisatore*, "*questo mi darà tempo sufficiente*. If my time has come to depart, so be it.''

Charsky, deeply moved by the Italian's unexpected sense of honour and reckless courage, jumped to his feet, from the trunk where he had been perching, and bowed.

"In that case, do me the honour of allowing me to be your second. Leave the arrangements to me."

The Italian had jumped to his feet also, and was standing at the window, facing its frozen blankness. When he turned, it was as though, the decision having been made, all his cares had fallen away from him; he looked suddenly serene, even cheerful. Charsky promised to return in the morning to inform him of the arrangements he would make with the Count's second; but the *improvisatore* told him not to trouble himself to come again, since there were many things he must do. Charsky nodded his head in sympathy, foreseeing that the Italian would be writing letters far into the night. "Very well," he said, "then I shall call for you at three in the afternoon."

The Italian, who had taken from his pocket his little picture album and was turning the pages with a wistful look on his face, replied distractedly: "*Molto bene. Grazie, Signor.*"

· (IX) ·

Of what use are you, days? The earthly world will not change its manifestations. . . .
BARATYNSKY

Having enjoyed little sleep for several days and nights, Charsky was by now almost dropping with fatigue. He even nodded off for several minutes in the sleigh taking him to the residence of the gentleman designated by Count O—— as his second. During his brief sleep Charsky had time to dream of five fox-cubs mewling and crawling round in the undergrowth of a forest, abandoned and hungry. The dream made him determined, on waking, to make another effort to deflect such an absurd duel. Count O——'s second, a Frenchman, proved to be a civilized individual, who was as anxious as Charsky to find a peaceable solution.

Together they drove to the Count's residence. It was past midnight, and they found the elderly gentleman ready for bed. He was wearing a silk dressing-gown open almost to the waist, the grey hair of his chest contrasting strikingly with his glossy black locks. He listened to their arguments, and at last agreed to accept an unwritten apology.

"We will make sure that you get it," said Charsky with relief.

The two seconds drove off to the *improvisatore*'s lodgings. They decided *en route* that Charsky should simply ask the Italian if he was sorry for the Count's distress. The moment he uttered a word which could, however liberally, be construed as regretful, they would leave again at once, without taking the risk of further discussion.

They found the *improvisatore*'s door locked, and it was a long time before their loud knocking could rouse him from sleep. Charsky was forced to shout through the door his message that he had further news from the Count: that he was now prepared to accept a simple expression of regret.

"I don't care," the Neapolitan responded in an irate

voice. "Please go away. My cold is much worse."

"Are you sorry the Count is so upset?" shouted
Charsky.

"No, I'm not! He's a fool! Tell him he's insulted
me! . . ."

"Very well, then," Charsky shouted angrily. "If you
want to throw your life away, there's no more to be
said."

The door stayed closed; the *improvisatore* made no
further sound; Charsky and the Count's second
withdrew cautiously along the corridor and down the
stairs. They directed the coachman to the Count's
residence. A surly footman in a nightgown and nightcap
promised to wake his master early with the news that the
duel must proceed.

Over a late supper in Charsky's study the two seconds
drew up the following conditions:

1. *The adversaries shall stand at a distance of twenty paces,
each being five paces behind his barrier, and the barriers being
placed ten paces apart;*
2. *Each shall be armed with a pistol; at a given signal they
may move up to but not beyond the barrier, and fire;*
3. *It shall be further stipulated that once a shot has been
fired, neither adversary may alter his position, so that the
person who shot first shall be exposed to his opponent's fire at
the same distance;*
4. *If both parties have fired without result, the procedure
shall be repeated, with the adversaries being placed at the
same distance of twenty paces and the barriers and other
conditions remaining as before;*
5. *The seconds must be the intermediaries in any*

communication between the principals on the field;
6.   *The undersigned, witnesses invested with full powers therefore, undertake upon their honour to ensure the strict observance of the conditions set forth above, each for his principal.*
27 January, 2.30 a.m.
(signed) VICOMTE D'E——.................................
Chargé d'affaires ....
C. P. CHARSKY...
Civil Servant of the 7th Class ....

Having snatched a couple of hours' sleep on his sofa, Charsky rose before dawn, bathed, perfumed, and put on fresh clothes. After answering some letters he drove to Kurakin the gunsmith's, and from there to the Vicomte's to check that all was in order from the Count's point of view. He returned home, ate a light midday meal, and changed again into formal clothes.

At a few minutes before three, his sleigh pulled up at the wretched inn. His legs heavy with weariness, he climbed the murky stairs and walked along the corridor. When no one answered his knock, he tried the door and found it unlocked. Inside, there was no sign of the *improvisatore*; nor, indeed, any sign that he had ever been there. His trunk had gone. The room was bare.

Charsky discovered from the landlord that his guest had paid his bill a few hours earlier and moved out, saying that he was returning home.

Fuming inwardly, scarcely able to believe the Italian's cowardice, Charsky had himself driven along the sombre banks of the Neva. The snow lay deep; a harsh wind blew in from the sea. The sleigh headed for Chernaya Rechka.

He decided he would offer to take the *improvisatore*'s place. That was the only honourable course. He looked for passing sleighs, hoping he might catch sight of some friend reckless enough to act as his second on the spur of the moment.

He saw a sleigh, at last, speeding towards him across the dark snow. The travellers, drawing close and passing, signalled to him to stop. Charsky recognized the Count and his second. The young Vicomte climbed out of their sleigh, and trudged through the snow back to Charsky. His face, under the fur hat, was paler than the snow.

Charsky expected him to ask why the *improvisatore* was not with him, but instead the gentleman exclaimed, in frightened tones: "We must call it off. Someone was there before us. The police are everywhere. One of my countrymen . . . d'Anthès . . ."

"What about him?" demanded Charsky, feeling an icy hand begin to clench around his heart.

"Wounded. Not severely. But his opponent . . . Pushkin . . ."

"My God!"

Charsky cried to the driver to turn round and head back to the city as quickly as possible.

No, this can't be! This isn't what I'd intended! If only he had listened to the cool and frivolous Charsky, instead of the disordered, emotional *improvisatore*, it would not have happened! Who cares if d'Anthès was screwing his wife? I run back through the pages of my notebook, frenziedly striking lines through the pages. I will start afresh, set the story a dozen years earlier, and manage the affair differently. . . .

· (EGYPTIAN NIGHTS, IV) ·

Or is all this a dream? Is all our life
Nothing but an empty dream, heaven's jest?
THE BRONZE HORSEMAN

When the Neapolitan had finished his performance, the applause hushed and the audience gone, Charsky invited the visitor to take a drive with him through darkened Petersburg. All the way through the silent streeets, he kept up a stream of compliments, assuring the crestfallen Italian that no one blamed him for having lost the thread of his improvisation on the theme of Cleopatra. "It was most unfortunate," explained Charsky, "that you were disturbed by those officers leaving. These are difficult days, with the old Emperor not long dead and the new one not yet crowned. Though in a way, the interregnum has helped us. Fewer would have turned up if the Court was not in mourning, if the usual balls and routs were going on. . . . But what do you think of Petersburg? Can you believe it was under water, just a year or so ago?"

They had entered a large and deserted square. "Who is

that on the horse, Signor?" asked the Italian, pointing at a bronze statue.

"That is our Peter, who founded the city. A year ago he was rearing his steed up out of the flood waters. It was an amazing sight."

"At least you need not fear fire, *Eccellenza*," the Neapolitan remarked with a merry smile. "As we do in Naples."

"That's true," said Charsky. "Our Neva and her granite are friendlier than Mount Vesuvius. We leave fire to our friends in Moscow. But I assure you, floods can be just as devastating. It was madness to build a city here. But what a splendid Idol he makes, don't you think? The monarch of half the world, or perhaps more than half. My old school friend Pushkin – you've heard of him?"

"*Si*, Signor."

"Of course! If he hadn't been in country exile you'd have gone to him asking for help, instead of me. . . . No, don't apologize!" Charsky smiled at the *improvisatore*'s obvious discomfiture. "You'd have been quite right. He's far better than I, a wonderful poet."

"Why is he in exile, Signor?"

"For writing libertarian verses; and scurrilous ones too, like his epic proclaiming that the Virgin Mary was fucked by God, Gabriel and Satan, all on the same day." Seeing that the Italian looked not in the least discomposed, Charsky added: "And because he himself was fucking a general's wife. If it weren't for these peccadilloes, he'd be with us in Petersburg tonight, instead of languishing on his family estate." Charsky sighed.

Observing that the Italian had lost interest and was no

longer listening, he went on: "Still, it's an ill wind that blows no one any good: thanks to the flood, I have been able to find you decent and cheap lodgings. The landlady is glad to have a new tenant. Her previous tenant is presumed to have been drowned in the flood, and she has been unable to find a replacement."

They had stopped alongside a row of elegant houses overlooking the square. Charsky prepared to alight.

"Is this where I am to live?" the poor Italian stammered, his eyes wide in astonishment. "And cheap, you say? *Corpo di Bacco!*"

Charsky chuckled as he assisted the Italian to alight. "No, my friend! I'll take you there tomorrow. It's in a modest neighbourhood, but clean and respectable. You'll like it. This house belongs to a noblewoman, the Countess Agrippina Zakrevsky. She is the most beautiful woman in Petersburg, as well as the most intelligent and the most indifferent to gossip. A veritable Cleopatra, a copper Venus! A previous engagement prevented her from coming to hear your performance, but she is most anxious to meet you, and hopes that she may be able to persuade you to perform for her privately. Her mother and younger sister were present tonight: you must have noticed them. The young woman wrote down a theme, at her mother's bidding. The poor girl is much in her sister's shadow."

Charsky and the *improvisatore* had been admitted to an elegant reception hall; the footman who took their coats and hats greeted Charsky with respectful familiarity, and said that his mistress was expecting them. Charsky led the way up a marble staircase.

"I am sure you will lose your heart to her," he said,

pausing to take breath before climbing another flight. "She is widely known as 'Cleopatra'; hence you may have noticed that her sister was the object of malicious glances and whispers when it was thought she might have proposed the theme of '*Cleopatra e i suoi amanti.*' It was my fault, and I did my best to rescue the situation. I have to confess that I had the Countess Agrippina in mind in writing down that theme."

Reaching an oak-panelled door, Charsky knocked and then opened it without waiting for an invitation. The room was empty. The Italian stifled a gasp of wonder at the magnificence of the Countess's drawing-room; though Charsky had always regarded it as remarkably austere, kept deliberately so by its mistress in order to heighten the effect on visitors of her own beauty. Tonight, however, his mind flashed to the poor room he had inspected that afternoon on the *improvisatore*'s behalf, a room which still contained the pathetically few belongings of its last tenant, a humble clerk. His life, even if he had survived the flood, could only have been laborious and mean.

Yes, sighed Charsky to himself, something must be done about it. Tomorrow there must be a new beginning. There's no other way. . . .

An inner door opened and the Countess entered. She glided towards Charsky, smiling, and held out her hand to be kissed; then she turned towards the Italian, who stared at her with an expression of awe, as though at an incarnation of the Virgin.

The Countess was in her late twenties. She wore her raven hair piled high and coiled; her face, with its high cheekbones, was a perfect oval. Her black eyes flashed provocation at the Italian, mockery, sorrow and desire — all at first sight, and all at once. Her red lips were inviting — full and exquisitely curved. Her bosom swelled over the décolletage of her white dress. The Neapolitan broke into a sweat, and he felt his heart racing. "*Madonna mia!*" he exclaimed, and then blushed and stammered an apology. The Countess burst into a pleasant laugh, and offered him her hand.

Charsky excused himself, saying that regrettably something urgent, requiring his attendance, had cropped up. He promised the pale, sweating *improvisatore* that he would return for him in a couple of hours. Charsky took his leave of the Countess and hurried from the room.

Hours went by, and Charsky did not return. It was morning before the *improvisatore*, unsteady from lack of sleep, found his way down the marble stairs and out into the fresh, cold air. A few flakes of snow drifted down. Instead of the huge and empty square which he had anticipated, he found himself gazing at a multitude of soldiers, foot and horse, drawn up in silent ranks. The *improvisatore* stopped, astonished, at the top of the granite steps. Unaware that he was looking down at the field of history, where the revolt of the Decembrists was about to be mounted and crushed, he stared entranced at what he took to be a ceremonial display. Bright sunlight flashed off helmets, breastplates and swords; gay plumes swayed above the sea of heads. Directly in front of the Countess's house was a clear space, a corridor some twenty paces wide, stretching to the other side of the square. Across this empty space, the bright regiments faced each other, motionless, silent.

The Italian noticed, beneath him and to the right, a

group of civilians standing among soldiers on that side where the ranks were thinner; and in their midst he recognized Charsky. Believing these civilians to be privileged spectators of the ceremonial parade, the *improvisatore* scampered down the steps, as fast as his tired legs would allow, and strode in their direction. A mounted guardsman from the loyal ranks came galloping to intercept him. The officer lifted his sword high, intending the rash intruder nothing but a warning blow on the shoulder; but his mount slipped on the ice, altering the direction and increasing the force of the blow, and the Italian's dismayed head parted from his body.

· 5 ·

"So this is where you've been! Don't tell me you've been up all night? A splendid honeymoon!"

I look up from the billiard table to meet Finn's yellowish smile. "Is it so late?" I ask. I notice that light is streaming in through the portholes, and when I glance at my watch I see it's 6 a.m.

"I'm sorry, am I interrupting?" he asks, his gaze falling on the notebook. "A story? Shall I leave you?"

"No, it's okay. I was just killing time. I couldn't sleep." I clamber off the table, and flex my stiff limbs. "You're up early," I remark. The old man gives a sigh. "I couldn't sleep either. Would you care for a game?"

I nod. "Billiards, pool or snooker?"

"Snooker, I think, don't you? It's somehow more sociable, and less skilful."

I get the triangle to position the reds. To my irritation he picks up my notebook and starts leafing through the last few pages. "I suppose I'm very old-fashioned," he says, "but I've never seen the need for bad language. Surely it isn't what we expect from literature? Sholokhov doesn't require such words in *Quiet Flows the Don*. Or, for that matter, Hitler in *Mein Kampf*."

Losing the toss, I break. Applying side, I scrape past the outlying reds of the triangle and spin off the cushion to nudge safely into the back line of reds. It's my one sophisticated touch, technically stupid, but it impresses Finn. "You obviously can play!"

"I haven't touched a cue for years. I played a little when I was young."

"A misspent youth." He chuckles drily, and bends over the table.

The old man applies unexpected, almost unimaginable, violence to his stroke and sends the red balls hurtling at lightning speed in all directions. They flash around the cushions so many times it's hardly surprising that two of them eventually settle into pockets. He assures me it's a fluke, and continues to thump the cue ball with incredible ferocity. After one such tremendous blow he says quietly: "I fear I may have given you the wrong impression about the Jews. I was involved with them quite extensively. Proportionately more of my time was spent dealing with the gypsies, as I've said; but I was also at such camps as Dachau, Birkenau, Belsen, Auschwitz, Sobibor, Maidanek, Treblinka. It was not easy. People think it all worked like a well-oiled machine, but it wasn't like that. The system was often on the point of collapsing. We had constantly to improvise solutions. And it's all very well people taking a strongly moral attitude from this point in time; it's a very different matter when you're in the thick of it, trying to do your best in very difficult circumstances."

The black, on which the game hinged, was resting against the baulk cushion. He doubled it flukily into a middle pocket with one of his violent, seemingly aimless blows. "I don't remember very much about those times. Old age, my dear Victor! 'Who now remembers the Armenians!' Hitler once remarked to me; and of course it's true, in a general sense. But personally I recall events early in my life much more clearly. Belsen is very blurred, but the plain of Maskinah is still vivid to me."

We strolled the deck for a while. Breakfast didn't begin till seven, half an hour away. We leaned over the rail at the stern. The rising sun glistened on the water. I noticed some brown fins trailing the ship, and pointed them out. "Yes, tiger sharks," he said. "Scavengers." His face expressed revulsion.

"It's the first time I've seen sharks in real life," I said, feeling excited.

"That's a mako over there – look! The blue one!" He raised the arm he had outstretched, changing the act of pointing into a gesture of affectionate greeting. "Now there's a shark! Brave, fast, aggressive. They call it Blue Lightning. It doesn't eat garbage like tiger sharks. The tigers are waiting for the galley to unloose the waste. They will eat anything – turtles, humans, excrement, tin cans, lumps of coal – and of course each other. I once saw a mako, hoisted high on a boom, savaged by a tiger shark that leapt right out of the sea and tore its belly out. I actually saw it bolt the liver, which must have weighed all of forty pounds. They're obscene creatures."

I gave a shudder; and said I thought I'd rest in my cabin for an hour before thinking of breakfast. The old man laughed, saying he was sorry if he'd put me off my fried eggs.

"Or liver," I added wryly.

I feel too unwell, not only for breakfast but for lunch too. I read a little, and drowse. Anna comes to see me, bringing grapes and some more cans of beer; but I'm not interested in beer, I want her to fill my hot-water bottle and bring me a flask of hot coffee. Then, in the afternoon: Nayirie. She wishes to discuss our arrangements for the divorce. Her bad Russian gets in the way of talking, but I discover she can speak quite good English, and we converse in that language. I find that she is pro-Soviet – a Marxist. The news angers and horrifies me. I haven't quit my prison, for a spell, in order to get tangled up with a Marxist bitch. "You should be emigrating to Russia, not America," I sneer. "But no doubt you want the capitalist goods – and freedom to shout your mouth off – while retaining the moral superiority of rejecting those values! I guess your Marxism is another thing, like the drug-smuggling, you forgot to put down on your application form!"

We argue fiercely. We even argue about Armenia – which is a bit of a nerve on my part, since I've never travelled further south than Georgia. Mandelstam's *Journey*, which I've read in *samizdat*, doesn't tell me much about the country; only that he loved their splendid intimacy with real things – pots, pans, and so on – and their strange aversion to ideology and clocks. Well, he should have met up with this ideological, clockwork bitch!

Paradoxically she is against the recent killings of Turks by Armenian terrorists; whereas I argue that it's perfectly understandable. "They only want the Turks to *admit* there was a holocaust. It doesn't seem much to ask!" She counters, "Where will it end?"

But mostly we fight over feminist issues and Marxism. I detest her narrow rationalism. I thought Armenians were supposed to be religious; the first Christian state. This bitch hasn't a spiritual bone in her javelin-throwing body. I find our fray stimulating, however, and remind her – half in sarcasm, half seriously – I haven't yet enjoyed my married rights.

"I was thinking that too," Nayirie said.

Feeling a flicker of triumph that the rationalist bitch is attracted to me, I pull her down to me and kiss her. She quickly detaches herself from my embrace, and goes to the door to click the lock. She undresses in a robot-like manner, as though taking off her tracksuit for a competition. Pumps, socks, dungarees, white unisex briefs. . .

Yet her body, when she climbed in beside me, was surprisingly fresh, soft and tender. Her limbs and breasts flowed around me like water, yet remained firm and full to touch – unlike Anna, there was something to hold on to. Her oriental skin sweated profusely; in no time, her breasts and belly were filmed with sweat, her own as well as mine. She gave out an acrid, penetrating odour which I found both revolting and exciting. Most striking of all was the luxuriant mat of pubic hair, jet-black and so cleanly defined it might have been sewn on to her skin. I could hardly take my eyes from it. Fondling her strong, plump thighs I said, "I could never love a Communist." "You prick," she hissed, and buried her fiery tongue in my mouth.

I climbed on top of her and penetrated. A stab for my father. A stab for every victim of Stalin, I thought. This bitch wasn't going to get away with a gentle screw. I'd fuck her till she screamed: "*Dostatochno*! No more! *Pojal-'sta!*" Her head was drumming against the pillow; the sweat poured from her face, her short black hair was drenched with it. I wouldn't give her the satisfaction of coming in her, but pulled out, held the seed, and buried my face between her thighs. Stretching my mouth as wide as it could go, I plastered it against her sopping cunt, my teeth biting her. Then I lifted my face from it and howled like a wolf; I bit her cunt again, and howled again. Her eyes were clenched tight, her lips drawn back in a grimace; the muscles of her neck and shoulders stood out, as if she were in the act of throwing the javelin. . . .

T·W·O

A BLACK LIMOUSINE PULLED UP OUTSIDE THE AIR terminal, and a uniformed driver leapt out to open the rear door. A tall, lean man emerged, wearing a Canadian lumber-jacket, an open-neck shirt, and grey trousers, with a Castro hat perched jauntily on his head of shoulder-length silver hair. It was the poet Victor Surkov. He was followed, more slowly, by Bliudich, historical novelist, Secretary of the Writers' Union in Moscow.

Having checked in, Surkov went to make a couple of phone calls. As he said cheerio to his wife and mistress, he had the sick feeling that he would never hear their embittered voices again. It was simply the awful fear of flying, which had only overcome him during the past year or so.

Surkov grimaced as he left the booth. Vera had put little Petya on the phone (though Surkov had said goodbye only a couple of hours before), as if to reproach him with his son's prattling innocence; and his girl friend, Tanya, had left silences where a child's voice should have been. Just as, once upon a time, before his first – the Marilyn Monroe – trip, his wife, Yevgeniya, had put little Katya on the phone; and Vera, his mistress, had reproached him with silences.

He joined Bliudich in the departure lounge. The old man's wrinkled yet characterless face, a kind of yellow-white disc, seemed somehow detached from the rest of his body, which was hidden under a fur hat, a black greatcoat and trousers, and polished black shoes. The old man suggested a drink. There was time.

Surkov was glad to sit again. Even carrying his heavy case a short distance had made his limbs feel shaky. He was on the mend, but still not entirely well. He fumbled in the pocket of his lumber-jacket for his phial of antibiotics, and swallowed a capsule with his vodka. "You'll start to feel better once you're over there," the old man remarked. If there was a sardonic overtone, Victor ignored it. The puckered anus in the centre of the Secretary's face opened into an attempted smile as he teased Surkov about the women waiting to fall upon him in New York. Victor smiled faintly in response. He briefly ran over with Bliudich some points about the travelogues he was to write during his trip, for publication in *Oktyabr*. He asked the old man if he liked the title *New York–Mexico–Havana*, and after a moment's reflection Bliudich nodded.

The flight was announced, and the two men stood up. They shook hands, and Bliudich wished Surkov a good tour.

He stood in line to be scanned and frisked, then walked with the other travellers down the long echoing ramp to the boarding area. Flight-phobia made him feel he was gliding effortlessly. It must feel like this when you're being taken to be shot, he thought. Round a bend at the end of the ramp were the exit doors, and seats which were by now almost filled. Victor sat down, again happy to rest. In contrast to the noise of the departure lounge, there was complete silence here. All the people, thought Surkov, had the same premonition. The tail of the jet that would carry them to their death could be seen through a window. Perhaps they had all had warning dreams last night; if they would only reveal their fears to their neighbours, everyone would turn back and go home. But each imagined that he alone had had a dream, and so believed his terror was irrational.

In the silence of waiting, invisible high heels came echoing, clicking, down the ramp; round the bend appeared three women, hurrying like Furies, the young woman in the centre being almost dragged along in the grip of two women in uniform. Surkov thought she had been caught trying to smuggle a weapon aboard; or maybe she was a dissident being expelled. Then he saw that she was blind. The air hostess guided her to a vacant seat and put into her lap her collapsible white stick and her handbag. The hostesses pushed out through the swing doors.

The blind woman held her hands in her lap, clasping handbag and stick, gazing straight in front of her. She was blond and good-looking. Victor looked at her with compassion and admiration, thinking, How wonderfully Russian she is! She straightened her coat hem; fumbled in her bag as if to make sure she had her travel documents safe; clicked the bag shut; stared again into space. Victor admired her self-possession, her air of being sufficient unto herself. She surely knew that everyone was looking at her, but she gave no sign that their morbid curiosity bothered her. Victor could imagine lying with her, stroking the soft pad of flesh beneath her chin. She would not know when he was about to kiss her. It would be strange, but not unappealing, to make love to a blind woman. While they sat together in the evening, listening to records, he in his armchair and she in hers, he would steal across the carpet to her, to reach up under her skirt, and she would jump with pleasurable shock.

Actually, she reminded him a little of Masha, his first wife; and Victor's heart saddened. Only, of course, she hadn't been blind – her brown eyes sparkling as she danced so swirlingly, so provocatively, at their University hops! Maybe they should have stuck it out, he thought. If only he hadn't played around, if only Masha had been more tolerant when she'd found one of Yevgeniya's stockings under their bed – the night she'd had to leave in such a hurry. But everything was stern in those days, the last before the Khrushchev thaw. Masha, during their courtship, had fought the bridgeheads under her rustling skirts (*they* weren't stern) as fiercely, and in the end as victoriously, as if she had been Leningrad fighting off the Nazis. Although she was all the time panting to let him in. Nothing, reflected Surkov, had ever matched that frustrated passion. He closed his eyes, trying to recall the cherry scent of her hungry and evasive lips. He wondered what had happened to her. With a sigh, he opened his eyes.

When the passengers had tired of looking at the blind woman, several of them returned to their covert inspection of Surkov. They recognized him from photographs; at least a couple of the passengers had been to hear him read – they had said so when they had approached him in the departure lounge to ask for his autograph. Though he had been a slightly disreputable minor celebrity for more years than he cared to remember, public inspection still embarrassed him. People would think him much older than he looked in his photos; especially now, after his illness.

At fifty, Surkov knew he was attractive to women still – or even more than ever. By watching his diet, spending an hour at the ice rink every day, and never conquering the habit of smoking, he had retained his lean figure; indeed, because of his illness he could do with putting some weight on. His face looked suitably ravaged for a poet. Women even liked his nose, so badly broken in a youthful skirmish that not even the grave would correct its hump. They even loved his long, curly silvery hair; but Surkov hated catching sight of it in the mirror. He would think: Who's that elderly man? He had for a few years dyed his fading hair; but then had forgotten to do so for a couple of months when he was unusually absorbed in work, and by then it was too late. It seemed to everyone that he'd gone grey almost overnight. People had stopped him in the street and asked him if he'd been ill. But away from a mirror, Surkov still believed his hair was black, and that he was not fifty but thirty.

The swing doors were thrown open, and everyone began to move towards the exit with the quietness of cattle going into a slaughterhouse. Victor looked at the blind girl, to see if she needed assistance; but her neighbour had grasped her by the arm.

The first-class compartment was almost empty; besides Surkov there were three American businessmen, and a Russian who looked like a diplomat, with his young male secretary. After the long slow taxi-ing, the thrust of the jets forced the poet back in his comfortable seat, and reminded him to get his teeth looked at while he was in New York. A few moments later he could light up a cigarette and look out of the window. Under the scattered cumulus clouds of a pleasant autumn day, Moscow was diminishing beneath him.

The hostess brought him vodka and the lilac scent of her skin as she bent close to his face. Surkov began to feel better.

The film, for the six passengers in first class, was Polanski's *Macbeth*. He listened to the English words through headphones, but the atrocious subtitles kept getting in the way, making him wince and occasionally smile. If they'd only had the sense to use Pasternak's translation. His mind flashed to the open coffin at Peredelkino, the grey-suited man's stony face, still youthful at seventy. Surkov had bent quickly to kiss his brow. Zina, the widow, and his long-time mistress Olga weeping, in separate parts of the crowd . . . Lara, who was both and neither, unnoticed in the throng . . . Someone reading "Life is not so simple as to cross a field. . . ."

Victor gazed out of the window at the serene empty sky above the polar white, and saw a shadowy face glancing in. The reflection disturbed him greatly. He felt horrified by his closeness to the airless ether, and knew that at any moment the plane would strike disaster – probably a direct hit with a jet coming from the opposite direction; at best he would be plunging towards the Atlantic; at worst, engulfed in flames, or his whole life wiped out without his knowing it. He dragged his eyes back to the film. With trembling fingers he lit a cigarette, though he had just stubbed one out, and swallowed a penicillin capsule with a gulp of vodka martini. He decided it was useless trying to cut down his smoking while he was on tour; instead, he would cut it out completely if and when he got back to Moscow.

He tilted his chair back, closed his eyes, and managed to control his fear by thinking of his situation back home. He was in a mess. What should he do? Free will, if it existed, was a doubtful blessing. Better, he thought, to be projected beyond the circles of the moon, as the Decembrists had been; and if a woman followed to share the hardship, she deserved all one's love. Some of the wives and sweethearts of the Decembrists had surprised everyone, themselves included, by their decision to embrace martyrdom for love.

Would anyone follow him if he were banished to the permafrost? Would Tanya? Vera, with Petya in her arms, wrapped in blankets? His Katya, scarcely a daughter any more? (She would only come if her mother could come too. Well, he still felt some affection for Yevgeniya and she had never remarried. . . .) Even Masha, wherever she was, might hear of his exile, and come. . . .

He saw their separate sledges, tiny black specks, arrowing in across the endless snow. . . .

Surkov opened his eyes, and gazed again out of the window, feeling now a mood of resignation to fate. Below him a host of white, fleecy clouds drifted, like icebergs in the ocean of air. The real ocean lay so far beneath, it could not be seen. Dreamily at first, almost serenely, lulled by the steady drone of the engines, Surkov gazed down and around him. But gradually fear, of a more impersonal kind, overcame him. How fragile, minute, meaningless was his life, flying over the great expanse; how minute this expanse, compared with the world; and how minute the world in comparison with . . . He thought of the philosopher and space pioneer Tsiolkovsky, who had hated death so much he dreamt of seeding the whole universe with people, all equally immortal. Where, now, was Tsiolkovsky, if not in his grave? Was it possible that there was somewhere *else*, some paradise in which Tsiolkovsky, and Surkov's mother, and his·father, the camp guard at Kolyma, shook hands with each other, greeted each other, ate, drank and slept together? Inconceivable! And God? To imagine a maker of this blue gulf, those fleecy clouds, was merely to compound the impossible. For it was impossible, logically speaking, for all this, including Surkov himself, to exist. Yet of course nothingness, also, was inconceivable. Moreover, the sky, the clouds, exhibited order and beauty. His consciousness already becoming American, Surkov recalled what an American, or perhaps English, astronomer had said, about the likelihood of chance producing the complex universe: that it was like expecting a tornado, blowing through a scrap yard, to create a Boeing. He's right, Surkov reflected. Darwinism doesn't explain it. To create all this mysterious existence, in only ten thousand million years – the merest blink of an eye! The spontaneous creation of order, like the *improvisatore*'s "Cleopatra"! No, I can't believe it. It may have happened by impulse, but it's not random.

Surkov listened to music, dozed, read and worked a little. When they glided down over the water towards Kennedy Airport, he felt only a little tense; and more because of meeting Donna Zarifian than because he feared he might never meet her. Would she live up to the photograph in the Yerevan journal which – together with photos of her sculptures – had made him write her a kind of fan letter? He had no doubt he would like her; but after the terrific build-up of their letters it would be a disappointment – to her especially, he felt – if there were nothing more than that. He recollected the passionate, often indecently erotic, letters he had written to her several months ago, usually late at night when he'd been working hard and was seeking relief in self-indulgent fantasy. She seemed not to take them too seriously, but you could never be sure what women really felt.

In the moments of cool fresh air between plane and terminal he breathed in deeply, and blinked against the dazzle of lights – for night was beginning to fall. Without tiresome delays he was shepherded to the VIP lounge. Flash-bulbs exploded; Surkov was embraced by Dave Abramsohn, his American agent, and they were good-humouredly disputing whether it was worse to have gone grey or bald. When they had finished pummelling each other affectionately, Abramsohn said, "There's someone here who also couldn't wait for your plane to come in – Mrs Preston." He moved aside, half turning; a short, stocky woman in a grey coat stepped shyly in front of Victor, wearing a nervous, awkward smile, blinking rapidly up at him through thick-framed glasses. To whom did this open, innocent face belong? What girl friend from the distant past? It took Surkov a moment to recall that Preston was Donna Zarifian's married name, and to relate the real woman to the photo in the Armenian journal. Then he said, "Well, at last! This is wonderful!" They shook hands, awkwardly. She was very short. Her anxious face craned up at Surkov. She enquired about his health, and he assured her he felt much better, after his last alarming note.

Dave told him some reporters were waiting to see him, assuring him they'd keep it brief; and Surkov, nodding, touched Donna on the shoulder and turned her in the direction of the interview room. The airport opened to him familiarly, despite the length of time since he had last toured. He recalled his very first trip – before it was Kennedy Airport. He had met Marilyn Monroe at a party: he could see her now, the blond hair, the innocent, ravishing face. He felt a stab of sorrow.

Victor sat on the table, poured himself a glass of water; laid out beside him his cigarettes and lighter; and smiled around at the dozen or so reporters. About half of them smiled back. He recognized from his last trip the ageing, careworn columnist from the *New York Times*, and let his eyes flicker round the others. The most attractive was a girl in a tailored suit who was probably writing a piece for her high school paper. He gave her an especially warm smile, and she blushed and dropped her gaze. He had instructed Abramsohn to invite such a girl.

Mr Surkov, welcome. How do you feel, being in the United States again?

I haven't really got my bearings yet. You must excuse my stupidity. I feel like it's a homecoming. I feel like I was born somewhere in the middle of the Atlantic, and this is my home as much as the Soviet Union. Well, I have been awfully lucky, I have been here three or four times, or maybe even five. Well, so I have been many times in my country!

Is there anything peculiarly American you're looking forward to again?

I guess ice cream and milk shakes! And watching the Dodgers play, yah? Well, also jazz. We have quite a lot of jazz in the Soviet Union now, but the standards are not so hot. Well, there is some good jazz but you have to know where to look for it. I'm looking forward to New Orleans, which is my next stop after New York. I've never been there. But I like an awful lot of things about American life. I don't really know what I'm looking forward to. Just feeling at home, yah.

What makes you feel so much at home over here?

Merely the people. The friendliness of the people. Everywhere, people are the same. Well, not precisely the same, of course, but the same friendly spirit, the same desire for peace. People are everywhere stockpiling weapons and everywhere they want peace. It's crazy.

Are you looking forward to meeting any particular friends again? Solzhenitsyn, for instance?

I would be happy to meet him. Well, there are very many friends I would like to meet, but there is so little time. I am only actually in the U.S. three weeks or so.

Do you think Solzhenitsyn would be happy to meet you?

Well, you will have to ask him. He is a very busy man. Or so I read in the papers.

In your biography of Sholokhov, you don't discuss the evidence, brought forward by Solzhenitsyn among others, that he stole most of And Quiet Flows the Don. *Why not?*

Merely because I don't see any evidence for this theory. Well, I don't think Sholokhov plagiarized. But of course he, in a way, didn't write it alone. I say that in my book. Merely because all art is a collaboration, a translation if you like. But plagiarism is a different matter.

It's ten years since you were last here, Mr Surkov.
That is correct.

And your last trip to the West was to England in 1972?
1972 or 1973, yah. You're right it was '72.

Why so long?
Merely because I have been very busy writing. I have been writing prose too, yah? and that takes up more time. I have made many trips abroad in the East – Poland, Czechoslovakia, the German Democratic Republic. Africa too, yah – I've been travelling a lot.

It's sometimes said you wrote the biography of Sholokhov as a penance for having requested political asylum when you were in London in '72. Is there any truth in this?
Well, I will show you how wide of the mark it is. As a matter of fact I was already writing that book before I went to England. I had started it already before I wrote my first novel, *Envy*, although I didn't publish it until much later. It took me a long time to write Sholokhov's life, merely because he has lived a long time, an unusually long time. . . . It's simply not true that I requested political

asylum. The explanation is really much more boring, yah? Simply, I got the news of my mother's death while I was in London. We were very close. She'd brought me up alone during the war and afterwards. So I was very upset. I was upset also because I had been out of the country when she died. Well, there were other problems too – domestic problems. So I simply didn't feel like going on with my tour. I holed up for a few days with some English friends, yah? and then I went back home. It was an invention of the English press that I asked for political asylum. I was suffering from something called mourning. Nobody understands this any more, or it's too boring an explanation.

Nevertheless, since then you've kept silent about infringements of the Helsinki Agreement. Why haven't you seen fit to support the dissidents, some of whom were your friends? – Sakharov, for instance, and Bukovsky?

I'm trying to give these up! . . . I did support. I have protested. The fact is that the so-called dissidents have gone about things rather crudely. It's not always been helpful. It doesn't always help to shoot your mouth off.

Some would see the anti-Semitic letter you put your signature to in Izvestia *as shooting your mouth off, and as not exactly helping the Jewish dissidents who are trying to get out. Why did you sign that letter?*

Merely because that letter wasn't anti-Semitic. It was anti-Zionist, which is quite another thing. It was pro-curing – uh, proclaiming – the rights of the Palestinian people. You see, if you'll permit me to say so, you over-simplify. These so-called dissidents are not always so innocent, not always so pure. In their motives, yah? Like, you have extremists here who wave banners and fight the cops, merely because they've got problems! They're freaked out! Well, maybe their cause is quite good – the oppression of blacks or women, yah? – but they're mainly protesting because they don't like living with themselves, they're screwed up! Well, we have screwed-up people in our country too! . . . Well, obviously I'm not saying the people you mentioned are screwed up, merely that it's not so simple, yah? If we sent them over to you, they'd drive you crazy, merely because they'd find something to moan about. They'd demonstrate outside the White House, and cause traffic pile-ups. Even in Stalin's time, people were sometimes unhappy for no reason, no reason to do with Stalin. Like, their hearts were broken, or something. There's a poem by Akhmatova, a wonderful poet who lived in bad times, and suffered a lot – well, you know about her; but in this poem, well it's only a few lines, she says, "What's war? What's plague?" – and by plague she means . . . yah? . . . these are transitional problems, they'll pass. The real terror is the flight of time. Simply getting old!

I'd like to bring up . . .

You see, the State, the political set-up, is often a cover for personal problems. Well, not precisely a cover, but – well, a lot of Russian writers have had pretty fucked-up personal lives. Kind of split in two, yah? Mayakovsky, Blok, Pasternak, Akhmatova even, Yesenin – they all had big problems. You can even take it back as far as Pushkin. Sometimes three people living and sleeping in one room. Merely because there was not much space in which to be unfaithful. Not Pushkin – Pushkin had plenty of space, but not enough time. You know, if he hadn't got himself shot over a dumb blonde, Pushkin might still have been alive during the October Revolution. Well, if he moved to Georgia, which he liked a lot. He would have been 118, but that's quite common in Georgia, as you know.

Are you saying . . . ?

I'm talking about the personal lives, the personal lives of our twentieth-century poets. What I'm trying to say is – if they were Americans you'd see them as some kind of freaks, or bums, like – I don't know – Scott Fitzgerald, Hemingway . . . I really don't know. But because they lived in bad times it gives them a kind of a, kind of a dignity. . . . If my country didn't exist you'd have to invent her, yah? And I guess we would have to invent you. Well, the only way I can explain it is the soft woman and the hard woman. In Pushkin's *Fountain of Bakhchisarai*, which is an early poem, in some ways a poor poem, the two favourites in the Khan's harem are a gentle Polish girl, Mariya, and a Georgian girl, Zarema, who's wild – you know, real hard, bitchy. Well, they are of course rivals. In the end their rivalry kills them both. But they are really only two sides of the same woman in Pushkin's mind, yah? Well, that's what I mean about the Cold War, about each side having to invent the other. Well, I don't really know if I'm making any sense. It's like a kid, yah? – a little boy. Well, I'm thinking of my little boy, who's delightful but a great trial. . . .

That would be your son by your third wife, Mr Surkov?
Yah, yah. Well, his mother is awfully soft with him, and

also awfully hard on him. He needs them both, yah? The woman who lets him snuggle up to her tits, and the woman who smacks him and puts him in his place. Well, of course he'd rather live with the one who lets him snuggle against her tits and put his head up her skirts. . . . It's not surprising, it's no big deal, the traffic is mostly one way from my country to yours. . . . Though that's not completely true, as a matter of fact: more people are moving back into Armenia, the Armenian Socialist Republic, than are moving out. . . . But in general it's true – most want the soft mother. But without the hard mother, the soft mother wouldn't be any fun. . . . That's what I'm saying. Well, I don't really know how to explain. It's like Rome and Alexandria, perhaps. Let's to billiards! Women playing billiards with eunuchs! Bored out of their minds, yah? And on the other side the Romans longing for the soft beds! Only East and West have swung round, yah? Well, it would simply be awful if my country and yours were the same. Just as if men and women were the same. Even if everyone is perfectly happy. Maybe especially if we are perfectly happy, yah?

Do the women in the Soviet Union tell you that your work is sexist? Has anyone let you know that?

Jesus Christ, I don't know what you mean.

I mean that you treat women as objects, as is obvious from your remarks about dumb blondes and tits, putting your head up their skirts, women taking on eunuchs. In your writings you conceal hatred for women under a guise of compassion, by constantly showing them as victims of violence. I just wondered if the women

in your country made you aware of how they feel about that.
Dave, I can't answer this shit.

What are you working on at present, Victor?
Well, I've just finished a long poem – not precisely a poem, more a novella, a *povest'*, about the Moscow Olympics. It's a couple of thousand lines, or perhaps a little more. It's really about the English runners Coe and Ovett. Well, in my poem I compare them to the Dioscuri, the heavenly twins. I was enormously impressed by them, but much more by the whole Olympics, which I saw. I was only sorry the Americans were not able to come. It was a pity.

Will you be reading this new work in New York?
Yah.

Will you be performing it from memory, sir?
Of course, yah.

Two thousand lines?
Well, it's about 2,300, I think.

Why do Russian poets have such good memories?
Well, it's not just the poets. It's merely because . . . well, first of all we are trained in the high schools to memorize, yah? It's a kind of a part of normal Soviet education. So, well, it triggers off an ability to soak in everything, everything you want. I don't really know how it happens. It's not only my own work, it's not merely an ego trip. I have in my head most of Blok, Pushkin,

Pasternak, Lermontov. Not merely the poetry but the prose also. Not the prose completely, but a lot of it. Also we don't know when it will come in useful. It's a kind of private publishing house, in your own head.

Do you mention Afghanistan in your new work?
No, it doesn't come into it. If one of your poets, Wilbur or Hecht perhaps, writes a poem about the Los Angeles Olympics, I guess they won't mention El Salvador, unless it's necessary to the poem.

What are your views on Poland? Do you think the Soviet Union will intervene?
My guess is, the people of Poland will resolve their own problems. I hope so.

You spoke earlier about the flight of time. You're now fifty, though you don't look it. . . .
Older, yah! . . .

. . . You've always been regarded as a young poet. How do you feel about being middle-aged?
I don't exactly feel middle-aged. Well, I feel quite old this last three, four weeks, merely because I haven't been awfully well. I don't really know how I feel. What hurts is not that you grow old but the world does. You stay the same, but the world gets older around you.

I'm not sure I get your meaning.
Well, like in the late Sixties, things changed a lot. Flower power, blue jeans, LSD, unisex fashions and hair styles, rock, hippies, the Beat poets, San Francisco, gays, yah? A

general cultural and sexual blurring. I was over here in '67, no it must have been early '68, and I saw it all happen. It was here first, yah? The world changed in that year, '68, and it was very disturbing. The world became older, in spite of the youth culture and mini-skirts. That's what I mean.

Most of your examples are very frivolous. How come?
I'm a very frivolous person – yah. Of course there were other things going on in '68, like the war in Vietnam. But I was asked what I meant by the world getting older, and I gave a straight answer. Blue jeans have affected people more than Allende or Nixon. . . . But I am frivolous, yah. Extremely superficial.

How do you react to being called the Kremlin's tame liberal?
I've never heard that expression. And now I'm awfully tired.

Thank you for answering our questions.
You're welcome.

Have a good trip.
Thank you.

Most of the way in from the airport the Russian lay slumped back in the passenger seat of Donna's car, his eyes closed. Now and then he opened his eyes and saw the stream of neon signs rushing by; and once, in his tired, dreamy state, he caught sight of a most dramatic sign, straight ahead, high above the expressway – a huge, golden moon. He was on the point of asking Donna what it was advertising when it occurred to him that it was the real moon. He pointed it out to her, and said, "It's bigger over here!"

She drove swiftly and erratically. Her old Dodge was far more dangerous than the Aeroflot jet, but he felt too tired and weak to care. Her gentle New England voice was soothing. It was a voice incapable of guile or irony, he thought. For instance, he had lingered after the press conference to talk to the sweet, shy, glamorous high school reporter. Without a trace of irony Donna was saying to him what a kind gesture that had been. Her real presence was confirming an impression he had gathered from her letters: that she was really quite innocent. Armenian women were by nature faithful, she had written. Surkov felt sure that her husband, from whom she had been divorced for five years, had been the first and only man in her life.

Except there was a mysterious friend she had never mentioned in her letters, called Krikor. If Victor didn't mind, if he wasn't too exhausted, he was coming round to supper to meet him. She had brought this up casually, when Surkov mentioned his desire to go to an Armenian church service. She had said she didn't often go (which had surprised him, since he'd imagined all Armenians were religious), but she had a friend who went regularly and would be glad to take him on Sunday morning. Her friend usually joined her for lunch, after the service, so it would be very convenient.

Catching sight of the moon again as it moved out of clouds above the Manhattan skyline, Donna said: "But the *poets* are bigger in Russia! Aren't you proud they actually went to the airport to interview you? That must be very rare."

"Don't be fooled by that," he growled. "They just remember the last time I boarded a plane in the West – in England – it was good theatre. A couple of rather burly friends on each side of me. And since then I've kind of disappeared from view. They weren't quite sure what to expect. Well, the fuckers didn't get much for their cab fares."

"I'm sure it wasn't only that."

They stopped twice during the journey. He needed cigarettes. She wouldn't let him get out of the car: he was not well, and she wanted to take care of him and make him rest as much as possible. He asked her to get a mild brand, and she came back with a carton of Carltons, which the man in the store had said were the mildest in the world. She wouldn't let Victor pay her for them. It was the first time she had bought cigarettes in her life. He knew she hated them, because her father had died of lung cancer. Victor found he had to struggle for ages even to light his cigarette, and when he had succeeded he found the taste, or rather no-taste, abominable. "Yah, it's very healthy!" he agreed, stubbing out the Carlton. She stopped a second time, and brought him back Marlboros, and again refused to take any money. Marlboros were stronger than he liked, but satisfactory.

She lived in a modern apartment block in half-derelict Brooklyn. She dropped him and his case off while she went to park the car, then joined him, smiling her nervous smile, weighed down by his heavy briefcase. Victor picked up his suitcase, muttered "Shit, it gets heavier," and followed her through the lobby. He was glad when the elevator had carried them up to her apartment and he could drop his case and sink into a deep soft sofa.

His tired eyes took in her spacious living room, which was neither surprising nor as he had imagined it; and also, under the bright electric light, he was able to observe his hostess clearly for the first time. Having hung up her coat, she asked him what he wanted to drink, and poured him a brandy; she put some gentle dance music on the stereo system, then went through into the kitchen. He heard dishes clattering. A few minutes later, she came back with a coffee tray. She poured their coffee and sat at his feet, tucked her loose-fitting blue skirt under her legs, and smiled up at him, blinking through the thick-framed glasses he hadn't known she wore. She forestalled his move to add cream and sugar. Her look of dog-like devotion started to irritate him; but he was grateful to be waited on, and it was clear that she liked waiting on him. He relaxed, beginning to realize that she would be quite happy simply to mother him for a while. Her only daughter was at graduate school, training to be an engineer. She had her own apartment.

At one time Victor would have been disconsolate to have heard of the mysterious Krikor, but now he felt relieved. Though Donna was attractive she was, simply, too old. In her photograph she had looked a ravishing twenty-five. As soon as he had learned she had a grown-up daughter, he had taken fright and had gradually lowered the emotional tone of his letters. He had become a little less evasive about his Russian commitments, hinting that his latest marriage, while in the process of dissolution, wasn't actually dissolved yet.

Seeing the sculptress in the flesh confirmed his doubts.

She was too old – he guessed, around forty-five. He knew it was illogical and unfair, having passed fifty himself. But he found it impossible to fall for women over thirty. He explained this to himself as his need to have women capable of growing and changing: like that delightfully fresh, well-dressed girl at the press conference. Besides, he simply didn't *feel* fifty.

Surkov also found it impossible to fall for women with thin legs, strident voices, or ideological commitment: whether to Communism or vegetarianism. Donna passed these tests: she had quite plump legs, a soft shy voice, and she was going to grill steaks for supper. From her letters he had already gathered that she had no political bee in her bonnet. She was just too old, and also too short. Though he could make love to her, he could not fall in love with her. It was a pity, he mused. He needed to fall in love again.

And I simply mustn't screw her, he thought, because she's clearly so vulnerable; and she's too nice to hurt. He could not imagine her small, gentle hands hammering the stone shapes that adorned the room and which, after he had finished his coffee, he looked at and admired. There was the abstract *Ararat*, of which he had seen only a photo. To his disappointment, most of her work was not especially suggestive of Armenia. The paintings were also not of a strongly national character, though most of their signatures were unmistakably Armenian. There were not even many books that bore on their spines the weird hieroglyphs of Armenian. The *New Yorker*, and two new American novels, lay on the coffee table. The apartment was as American as her accent.

She apologized for not asking him sooner if he needed

the bathroom, and said she would show him his bedroom after he'd finished his drink. She would go and call her mother. There had been burglaries in the building, so she liked to make sure her mother was all right. "You must use this place just as if you were at home," she said. "There's only one room you mustn't go in." She pointed to a door. "That's my studio. You must promise not to go in there." For a moment a proud, furtive look came into her eyes. "You must promise!"

"I promise! But I'm disappointed. I'd like to see you at work."

"Well, I shan't be working while you're here. But you mustn't go in. There's such a mess."

Victor relaxed with his brandy, flipped through the *New Yorker*, dipped idly into the novels, stroked a Siamese cat's thin disdainful head, and half-listened to Donna's phone call. The phone was in a kind of alcove, and it disturbed him that he could hear so much, even with a record on softly. He'd have to ring Moscow when Donna was out shopping. It seemed odd to him that Donna was ringing her mother, when she lived just three floors above her. Her tone to her mother was curiously polite and formal, almost as though she was checking to see if an old neighbour was okay.

He wondered if she still intended to sleep in her mother's apartment while he was there. She'd written that the Armenian community was very strait-laced, and it would never do for her to share the apartment with him at night. It had irritated him, and made him more determined to seduce her. He'd been tempted to write back, jokingly, that it might be more convenient for her if *he* slept with her mother! Now, it occurred to him that in fact that might not be a bad idea. Maybe he would get more out of the mother, old Mrs Zarifian: more of Armenia. She was actually Armenian, had lived in Armenia for the first few months of her life.

He still didn't know why he preferred not to visit Armenia itself, as he so easily could.

Donna had rung off, and dialled again. She spoke more warmly – he presumed to her friend Krikor, telling him they were back.

"Is your mother okay?" he asked, when she returned to him and sat in an armchair.

"She's a little tired. She's most concerned that you're not well, and worried in case you've come just so as not to disappoint me!"

They both smiled at the quixotic idea. "She's dying to meet you," she added. "You'll see her tomorrow, if you feel up to it. And Lucy's coming home to have tea with us, after her classes. She's also dying to meet you."

"That will be nice."

"You're sleeping in her room. Would you like to un-pack and freshen up? Krikor will be here in about half an hour."

"Okay." He tried to spring up with his usual vigour, forgetting that he was recovering from an illness; but had to sit back down again, for a moment. His legs felt weak, and his suitcase weighed a ton. He was glad to drop it again in the passageway. By ill luck he was standing opposite a full-length mirror and he could not avoid a glance at the ghastly spectre, before Donna removed it by pulling a handle and he saw that the mirror was screwed on to the bathroom door. She was telling him something about the hot-water system, and he nodded, too tired and confused to take her words in. She indicated the door to the right, and said it was hers. He believed she was telling him that she was not going to be sleeping with her mother after all; but again, since his head was spinning and she was mumbling somewhat and mixing it up with questions about what he liked for breakfast, he wasn't quite sure if he'd misheard.

Donna opened the door to the left of the bathroom, and held it open for him to pick up his case and go through. He dropped the suitcase and looked around. The room was in a mess, uncertain if it was Lucy's bedroom or Donna's storeroom. Lucy was all but gone. At least I was spared this painful stage with my daughter, Surkov thought sadly. Lucy had left only the things she didn't need any more: posters of pop idols she had grown out of; school sports gear piled in one corner; some tattered comic books on the shelves, propped between a forlorn teddy bear and Donna's sewing machine.

"Will it be okay?" she asked anxiously. "You know what teenagers are like. I'm sorry about this junk — if it's in your way . . ." There were cartons piled in the corner near the window.

"No, it'll be fine."

"I've emptied one of the drawers for you."

A framed photograph of two laughing girls in jeans stood on the chest of drawers. He asked if one of them was her daughter. She said yes, the girl on the left, and Victor observed that she was quite beautiful.

"Do you think so? Yes, she is, but you won't think so when you see her. She's cut all her hair off. Since she's the only girl in her department, she thinks she mustn't look like one."

"That's a crime."

When she had gone, Victor lay on the bed, smoking. His thoughts turned to the charming high school girl he had talked to at the airport. Would she come to his reading on Friday? With Donna hovering near it had been difficult to press home his invitation. Her image disturbed and excited him. Obviously she had gone out of her way to look smart for this thrilling experience, but it was more than that. She had the tailored elegance of the better-off Muscovite girls of the Stalinist years. It seemed to him that her young soul would be responsive to him; that she might, in fact, be the woman he had hungered to find all his life, with whom he could live in daily closeness and yet never cease to find exciting. Maybe he could persuade her to abandon school for a few weeks, and fly with him around the continent. He saw himself lying naked with her under the warm blue skies of Mexico and Cuba. She would not, surely, pass up the chance of such travel? He wished he could blot out the next two weeks. New York was as dreary as Moscow.

But would she respond, he wondered? It never ceased to infuriate him that such stylish girls usually passed him by, whereas the scruffy, thin lipped bluestockings fell at his feet in droves. The ideological bitches, like the one tonight who had tried to attract his attention by abusing him. As if they sensed, in his ravaged, absurdly spiritual-looking face, a kindred spirit, a serious, intense and lofty soul. It was crazy, but there it was. Only Surkov knew how light-minded he was: that he'd much rather have dinner with a dumb blonde in a tight sweater and stiletto heels than with the most intelligent, overalled dissident of the western or eastern kind.

Wishing he could go to bed straight away, without the

tedium of becoming acquainted with a stranger, Victor hauled himself from the bed and wearily started to unpack. He could hear the sounds of Donna taking a shower. That seemed a good idea. It might liven him up.

Surkov was further enlivened by the Greek taverna record chosen by Krikor. The steak was good; the wine too; and Donna, in a red silk dress, was quite attractive and sparkling. With her glasses removed, and smiling, revealing her even, white, all-American teeth, she shed twenty years. How strange, he thought, as she smiled at him between her rare nibbles of food and sips of wine: her eyes are young and beautiful, but she prefers to hide them behind those huge, thick-rimmed glasses. . . . And her teeth are also young and beautiful – and American; whereas her lips, closed, are dry and cracked, like her skin; as old as Armenia. But it was easy to see why the photograph had fooled him, for she had been smiling broadly in it. Surkov, even as he complimented her, had managed casually to mention the photo in the Yerevan journal, and she had satisfied his curiosity by explaining that it was only a snapshot Lucy had taken three years ago – but people had said she looked quite nice in it. "As nice as it's possible in her case," Krikor had agreed.

He was constantly putting her down, her Armenian friend, in a sardonic, affectionate way. Surkov took to him. He was a lawyer, in his late thirties, swarthy, moustached, and with the strong, hooked Armenian nose. He had moved to New York from Beirut, a few years ago, and his accent was Armenian still. His sense of humour was rough and cruel, yet there was an underlying gentleness about him. And Krikor, for his part, clearly enjoyed Victor's company. Tipping back his chair, a cheroot between his handsome white teeth, he listened with pleasure to the Russian describing his two doctors. . . .

"You see, I have two doctors," explained Surkov. "It's a group practice. I go to one if I have a physical complaint, merely because she's good, she knows her stuff. But she is grey-haired and extremely plain. I too am grey, I know that. Still . . . she is pleasant, but very prudish. I once went to her suffering from a rash on my balls, and a look of enormous relief crossed her face when she discovered it had spread, in a small way, to my armpits. She examined my armpits! But still, she cured my rash. Here too! My other doctor is young, just out of med school, an awfully good-looking blonde. She doesn't know much about physical ailments, but she's a marvellous listener if you've got problems. She keeps her other patients waiting for hours while she probes me for intimate details of my personal life. So I go to her when I need to talk to someone, and maybe get some more sleeping pills. It works very well! The only trouble is when I have physical and emotional problems together! Like maybe the fever I'm just getting over, I don't know."

"So which doctor did you go to for that?" asked Krikor.

"Well, actually I had no choice. I was laid up in bed, and my young blonde doesn't yet do house calls! My grey-haired one wanted me to go into hospital for tests, but I fear hospitals like the plague, and so I immediately started to feel better! She did a few tests in her office when I was well enough to go out. It seems I've still got some sort of blood infection. It was touch-and-go whether I came, but I didn't want to miss meeting Donna, I'm loaded up with two different antibiotics. But actually, it's just occurred to me that I feel really well, for the first time in weeks! I've even been off spirits, but I'm really enjoying a drink again tonight."

"That's wonderful," said Donna, her eyes sparkling at him and her hand lifting his brandy glass to refill it. The amount and variety of booze in her cocktail cabinet amazed Surkov. The reason, she explained, was that she gave many parties, and since she hardly touched drink herself she kept gathering bottles. In Surkov's hazing vision his hostess began to appear more and more pleasingly enigmatic. She was abstemious in all her habits, yet did not seem to mind if others weren't. Krikor and Victor were quite tipsy by the time she had poured herself a second glass of dry white wine. Surkov had sensed before, from her letters, a strange mixture of puritanism and tolerance – perhaps more than tolerance, perhaps even enjoyment – of others' excesses. She had responded to his lurid sexual fantasies with New England reserve, yet never once suggested that she was offended. And now, this evening, though her speech was as chaste as her written style, her companions' obscenities passed over her like sunlight across a lake.

"Holy shit!" Krikor exclaimed, when Victor told him about the accusation of sexism at the press conference. "You know what that bitch was doing? – she was trying to rape you." "I don't mind the Reaganite attacks," Surkov said thickly, "I expect that. I expected it as soon as I entered the room. If you're Russian, you develop a nose for such things. I can cope with the White Guard. It's the Marxist shits I can't take, the one-dimensional rationalists, the social engineers, the thin-lipped fanatics like that little humourless feminist fart. If she lived in Moscow she'd be out for my blood." Donna, her gaze moving serenely from one to the other, simply added: "I felt very angry at some of the questions. But you handled them beautifully, Victor."

"Well, they weren't so tough. It was the roughest questioning I've had in this country, but I'm used to worse. . . . People who wear their ass-holes in the middle of their faces. . . . Tonight was okay. Well, what I mean is, your English is pretty damn rusty, yah? You don't always grasp what they're asking, yah? And so you take it slowly, and they don't always catch your answer, merely because your English is poor; well, not precisely poor, but keeps changing direction, yah? . . ." Donna and Krikor laughed. "Then, of course, you can throw in a bit of Russian temperament, which they adore, like 'Dave, I can't answer this shit . . .,' glaring like Ivan the Terrible; and the women reporters wet their pants, even the Marxist feminists – well, *especially* the Marxist feminists, yah? . . ."

"I guess you're right," said Donna. "I guess you'll have my daughter falling for you tomorrow."

"Why, is she a radical? Oh shit!" He screwed up his face humorously. "You know, we have feminists too; but their aim is basically to restore the traditional role of women! I shall tell your daughter about them. They don't want to go down into coal mines. But of course they've been driven underground. . . ." He barked a laugh. "They're also religious, of course. I consider myself an ardent Russian feminist."

Victor started to stand up as Donna began clearing the table, but Krikor shook his head sternly and said, "That's

women's work. For Armenians, that's women's work."
The Russian was not sure whether he was serious or
joking, or perhaps serious-joking; but in any case Donna
also told him not to help. "He means it," she said, with a
wry smile, nodding down at Krikor.

Surkov still couldn't work out what was between them.
It roused his curiosity, quite apart from the fact that he had
made up his mind that it would be interesting, after all, to
go to bed with Donna. Not tonight, of course, but during
his stay. He watched Krikor studiously not watch Donna's
swinging hips as she carried a pile of plates into the
kitchen. They behaved towards each other as though they
were more than friends, but less than lovers. Had they
been lovers once, but were now friends? Were they friends
who couldn't decide if they should become lovers? Did
Donna wish them to be friends, and Krikor, lovers? Or vice
versa, though that seemed less likely? Surkov was baffled.

The sculptress came back with a platter of cheese and
biscuits and a pot of fresh coffee. She refilled their cups and
helped them to cream and sugar. She offered Surkov more
brandy and he said he would try some of her green
chartreuse.

She found an old Duke Ellington record for him, and
asked him if jazz truly wasn't so hot in his country; and,
more important, what else wasn't so hot? What was life
really like over there? He warned her not to be led astray by
the friendly correspondence she had had with Soviet-
Armenian curators when they had mounted the small
exhibition of her work in Yerevan. By all means she
should take up their warm invitation to visit; but not to
expect everything to be rosy. She seemed as innocent
politically as sexually. Of course, thought Surkov, it was

natural she should take a somewhat indulgent view of his country. It wasn't the traditional enemy, after all; it hadn't stolen nine-tenths of her land. Krikor's views were similarly naïve. These two would be glad of Soviet expansion in that region, and who could blame them?

The Ellington stopped. Surkov got up to turn the record over; and then stooped over his briefcase. He returned to the table with a sheaf of papers in his hand. "I'll show you something about my admirable homeland," he said. "Let me read to you from a piece I wrote about the English double agent, Philby, now living in Moscow. I submitted it to *Yunost'* and had it back yesterday, corrected." Surkov flipped over a couple of pages, then began to read, letting his powerful voice fade to a whisper when he came to parts which had been crossed through with an editorial pencil. . . .

"'Philby still looks every inch an Englishman, and throughout our conversation his love of his native land, the land of Shakespeare and Dickens, was evident. But he believes patriotism must yield to a still higher virtue. Truth and justice must come first, though it is never easy to overcome one's patriotic instincts. ~~Even Pushkin fell from grace, in this one respect, by seeking to justify, in his "Reply to the Slanderers of Russia," the Tsarist oppression of the Polish uprising of 1831.~~ Marxist-Leninism, unlike bourgeois ideologies, has always put internationalism before narrow self-interest.

"'There exists a snapshot which might have meant the end of Philby's career as a Soviet agent: a photograph in which he is standing, with a companion, against the background of Mount Ararat. His English paymasters should surely have noticed that their "spy" was not on the

Turkish side of the mountain, as they believed, but on the Soviet side! Why did he take such a risk, why did he allow the snapshot to be taken? Merely because he knew his English paymasters were ignorant of the topography! That was what Philby told me.

"'~~Well, it may be so, but I suspect a more interesting reason, hidden even from himself.~~ . . . Ararat – sacred peak to all Armenians!' – Well, here," Surkov interpolated in a normal tone, "the editor's scribbled in 'people of the Armenian S.S.R.! . . .' 'Fabled haven of Noah's ark! Ararat – stolen by fascists after the genocides of 1915 and earlier. . . . Now, the tiny segment of ancient Urartu, ancient Armenia, which survived the Young Turks is a thriving member of the Soviet community of republics; yet its people can never for a moment forget that their most holy place is in a hostile country ~~under the grip of military dictatorship.~~ "You, my mountain,/will you never walk toward me?" (Kevork Emin). More than a mountain – symbol of justice and freedom. . .

"'And so – Philby at Ararat! ~~Did not Philby wish to escape into its pure snows? Pure snow-white peak over sun-parched Armenia, and its ancient language, "whose boots are stone, it can never be worn out . . ." Weary of deception, didn't he yearn, like Mandelstam of an earlier generation, to cultivate a sixth, an Ararat, sense?~~ Wasn't he saying, through the revealing photograph: If only you were not blind, you would see which side I'm on! But these peaks dazzle you. . . .'"

The Russian poet dropped the sheaf of papers on to the floor. "Well, as you can see, our editors have become quite permissive!"

"I don't understand," said Donna, "why they've

thrown out the reference to the military dictatorship in Turkey? Surely that's right up their alley?"

Surkov chuckled grimly. "You'd have thought so, wouldn't you?" He stooped to gather up the papers, and straightened them. "Well, that's the most interesting cut. I was trying to check out something a friend of mine told me. He has a mistress who throws scenes, gives him a bad time. Her mother was an actress in the theatre of Meyerhold; and it shows. Well, she's been screwing around with someone pretty high-up, called Kozarsky. He's a kind of a 'dove,' and his conscience bothers him from time to time. He let on to my friend's girl that by the end of the year Poland will be under military rule. The Poles will do it themselves. Solidarity will be crushed. I'm telling you this in confidence. There's nothing you or anyone else can do about it. This friend of mine had been invited to go to Warsaw in December, and his girl didn't want him to get mixed up in anything bad, so she spilled the beans. This" – Surkov smote the manuscript with his knuckles – "backs up what Kozarsky said. These fucking editors know what's going to be sensitive."

"But Victor, that's awful," said Donna, screwing up her eyes in alarm. Krikor, too, nodded, his chair tipped back, cigar smoke sidling out through clenched teeth.

"So your fucking radicals better stop beefing about El Salvador and start worrying about Poland," growled Surkov.

Krikor shook his head. "Both, my friend."

They drifted into a debate on whether left- or right-wing dictatorships held the greater evil. Surkov argued that the Left was worse, since its philosophy was so all-embracing, and so rational-seeming, that it consumed body and soul. "You tell that to the Armenians who were wiped out by fascists in 1915," Krikor said, with a scowl. "Those bastards!" He proceeded to pour out a litany of genocide which had Surkov nodding and apologizing. Krikor urged Donna to show her guest her father's journal of the genocide; but Donna, embarrassed, her eyes lowered, said her father's English was poor and his hand-writing almost unreadable. She looked still more uncom-fortable and shamefaced when Krikor admitted that he didn't lose any sleep when an Armenian terrorist bumped off some Turkish official.

"What a fucking world," Surkov said, with a heavy sigh. He took a gulp of brandy, draining the glass. It tasted sweet. He realized he had poured and drunk a large brandy glass of green chartreuse by mistake. He asked if there was some coffee left. Donna said it would be no trouble to make another pot. She went through to the kitchen and Victor lurched out after her. He leaned against the door jamb and watched her while she put on the coffee, piled dishes into a machine – "The wonders of America!" he observed with a laugh – and wiped off the electric grill with a cloth. "I've brought a present for you," he said, in a voice he knew to be slurred.

"Oh? How nice! Where is it?"

"It's a poem. I'd like to say it to you. I hope I can remember it; in the Russian it's got rhymes, but I can't do that in English. It's just a rough translation. It's called 'In Two Countries'."

Then, as the quiet, middle-aged sculptress stood, watching the percolator, her head bent, her back turned to him, Surkov began to speak his poem, in a slurred voice

yet with the rhythmic, exalted tone he always adopted
when addressing his Muse. . . .

      "You write to say
      you write me letters
      in your sleep.
      Yes, but I want
      to run my fingers
      through your hair's
      black diaspora –

  "Well, it looked black in your photo, but I can see now
it's brown; but still beautiful . . .

      "where it falls away
      from your fringe;
      or just to
      feel it brush
      my skin. To look
      into your clear eyes
      and say – *Armenia*!
      Meanwhile, write to me
      from that room
      of Ararat snow
      above Manhattan,
      full of springs, stones,
      deserts, tangerine trees,
      grief, panthers
      and gazelles. Where else
      should an Armenian
      write letters?

"For night is where
you can live
in two countries.
And that other
native land
you have never seen
will grow dearer
each day you live
in another place
almost as dear.
Even though Armenia
no longer exists
you will of course
love it blindly,
transfusing the blood
of its heart
into stone.

"You are driving
to a late movie,
in reflective Manhattan –

   "Well, I don't know if you ever do that; it just fitted the
poem. . . .

"the sunset
is blinding. Here
it is deep night.
For some time now
I have had trouble
falling asleep.
Something wants me

to stay awake,
or to sleep
forever. It staggers
my heart,
makes me exhale
like a bellows
too quickly,
or stops me
from breathing in.
I have to get up, smoke,
call up some
erotic image
to cast that demon
before I can sleep
and write to you.

"Turning in bed
restlessly, you urge me
not to smoke so much,
recalling someone dear
to you who died
of lung cancer;
and I'm watching
a small child
startled by
a bird on the grass
beneath the white birches.
He totters towards it,
pointing, chortling;
it is the bird from
his picture book.
This is creation's

first bird, first child.
Upstairs, your mother
still can't sleep.
The bird flies off;
rain spurts."

"That's beautiful," said Donna. "Is that your little
boy? Is that Petya?"

"Yes, it is," Surkov said.

"You must have read,
in more detail than I,
about the violinist
at the Met, who
when she slipped out
in the interval
of the ballet *Miss Julie*,
full of scenes
of erotic violence,
was waylaid by
A Phantom of the Opera,
who stripped her,
tied her up,
and hurled her
down an air shaft.
Last night
as the Berlin Ballet
performed their other
piece, *The Idiot*,
police with dogs
combed the Met. . . .
The killer clearly

knew his way around.
Yet they think it's easy
being a violinist.

"It's not easy
even to be human
any more.
But you've helped me
to cling on by
the skin of my teeth,
with your carvings
of pure stone;
thank you for saying
in one of your letters
that the unicorn
was the only creature
to refuse the ark,
but struggled in the flood
for forty days
while everything else
was snug on Ararat.
You allowed me to see
its defiant horn
cresting the surges
of our bloodsoaked age.
Thank you for that."

Surkov stopped. His audience didn't say anything but
just stood over the percolator with her head lowered. He
came towards her and, putting his arm around her, drew
her in to him slightly and kissed her hair. "Thank you,"
she said softly. "It's a wonderful present."

The coffee was ready and they returned to the other room. After drinking a cup quickly, Victor said he would call it a day. Donna told him to sleep on as long as he liked in the morning; Krikor got to his feet, shook hands with the Russian warmly, and promised to call for him on Sunday morning to take him to the Armenian church. Surkov farted involuntarily; said, "I'm sorry"; and tried to steer as dignified a course as possible across the room to the door.

In the bathroom he chuckled as he swayed about the toilet. He felt, though drunk, well. He rejoiced in his recovered health. "Health is the only country that matters," he said, addressing the wavering jet of pale urine; and then he roared with laughter.

It was hot, that was the only trouble. He had not liked to ask Donna if she would turn down the heating. In the bedroom it was even hotter. He pulled back the curtain to open the window, but the window locks were unfamiliar to him, and he gave up. In any case, since they were six floors up it was better not to open the window; he might walk in his sleep. Clumsily he undressed, and with a sigh of pleasure stretched out naked in the cool sheets. It seemed days since he had been to bed.

He was confident that tonight he would not suffer from the breathing problems that attacked him before sleep. Drunkenness always seemed to relax him enough to keep that demon quiet. He lit the last cigarette of the day, and rested contentedly on his elbow, puffing slowly and letting his thoughts wander.

If Tanya should decide to quit, he reflected, can I survive? Well, I'll have to. If I could simply wipe the slate clean, as by a Biblical flood — then I'm sure we could make a go of it; but as things are . . . It would have to be with someone completely new, and young, on another continent. . . .

He heard the soft murmur of Donna and Krikor talking. What was the game between them? He would ask Donna point blank tomorrow. He stubbed out the cigarette in a saucer, switched off the light, and settled down, with a grunt of blissful pleasure. His thoughts drifted and were lost. When he opened his eyes, there was no light shining through the crack beneath the door; the silence was complete. Had Krikor left? He certainly hadn't heard him go. He was probably in bed with Donna. He was probably just across the hall banging the hell out of Donna. Pleasant giggles ran through Surkov's body, at the thought of all he had taken for granted and become agitated about.

The apartment seemed rapidly to be cooling. He had come awake because he felt chilly. He switched on the light, got out of bed, and fumbled on his pink striped pyjamas. He fell back into bed, pulled up around him the blankets which he had pushed to the foot of the bed, curled up tight, and fell asleep.

He slept deeply for a couple of hours; but then he began to toss and turn, and fling the bedclothes off him.

He woke with a start, and felt the hammer of a hangover strike him. He groaned, and let his head fall back quietly on to the pillow. The hammering eased. He could feel sweat pouring out; his pyjamas were soaked through and sticking to his body. But what an extraordinary dream, he thought. I ought to write it down. I'll do it in the morning. . . . Those two girls! I suppose they were Mariya and

Zarema, only Zarema became Armenian because I'm here . . . I'd love a long, long ocean voyage. . . . I'm going to have to get up, damn it, in a minute; need a piss, and my mouth feels like a Turkish brothel. . . . Well, that's fitting. Was the old man my father? I guess he was. But it wasn't entirely his fault. The camp guards were also victims of Stalin, in a way. The war brutalized him. . . . Also I don't think they got on very well, at least when he came back after the war. He was probably glad of any excuse to pack his kitbag again. Anyway, he paid for his crime . . . a Zek's knife in the guts is no more pleasant than a bullet in the neck. . . . Shit, this head! And I'm shaking all over again. . . . There's no fucking air in this room. . . .

Victor stretched up to turn on the light, but did not yet risk moving his head. It's amusing, though, he thought, that I imagined myself completing Pushkin's work! It's not the first time I've dreamed in verse, but never so clearly. . . . I ought to get it down in story form, as soon as possible. I need a secret place where I can hole up. I don't take to this room, it's so airless. . . . Hell, I've got a temperature, I think, and there's a pain. Yes . . . Christ, I hope it's not my liver. They're back again, the shakes. It was a mistake to come. The best thing I can do is go straight back home and get it sorted out. . . . Just as I did ten years ago! It's turning into a habit. . . . Oh well, fuck them. What time is it in Moscow? I can ring Vera up and ask her to make me an appointment at the doctor's; but maybe she's already dropped Petya at the nursery and gone to work? I've forgotten what the time difference is. I feel so ill I can't think straight.

Well, the first thing is a pee and a drink of water. Then I'll have a smoke and think out what I'm going to do. . . .

He hauled himself out of bed, his temples thumping.
Elvis Presley leered down at him. He stumbled towards
the door. Pushing it open, he came straight up against
another man in the passageway. The man, in striped
pyjamas, was about to pull open the bathroom door. The
encounter with Krikor was so shocking, in the blackness
lightened only by the glow from his bedroom, that Surkov
let out a horrified gasp. Krikor's face was also white,
shocked, and ill-looking – Victor was about to mutter an
apology, when his groping hand touched the mirror, and
the half-open bathroom door swung closed. He stood
panting, his left hand on the door handle. He put his other
hand to his heart, which was thumping wildly.
"Jesus! . . ."

When he was in bed again, naked, the light out, his heart
gradually quietened and he felt a little better. I must have
imagined the pain. And I don't think I've got a temperature, it's simply too damn stuffy in this apartment.

I really thought I was in for a heart attack. It wouldn't be
surprising. And what then? Death? – Are there any
cigarettes left in the crumpled packet? That's really the
only question. I simply must get this down on paper. And
for that I'll need somewhere peaceful, and a secretary. I'm
not ready for old Mrs Zarifian. I guess I'd better go
through with Friday's performance, as it's a big reading
and a big fee, and then I'll get the hell out. I'll tell Dave I
have to rest. It's true enough. I'll go straight on to Mexico,
and take that girl with me, if she'll come. Surely she will.
I'll find out from Dave tomorrow – no, today – what
high school she's at, and give her a call. She obviously
knows how to take dictation. I'll have to square my change
of plans with that shit Bliudich, but it'll be no problem. I

can still write my piece for *Oktyabr*. . . . "The gentle Armenian sculptress with whom I stayed was fearful for her mother's safety. The apartments where they lived had recently been burgled. . . . Longing to take up the friendly invitation, etc. . . ." No problem. I'll buy Donna a bunch of flowers.

With that girl's help, I think my story will come very quickly. Maybe only three or four days. The first honest thing since *Envy*. That was Sholokhov's biography, though none of the stupid cunts realized it, either here or there. I should have asked her her name, but Abramsohn will know who was there.

That village just south of the Arizona border . . . that's the place. I'll lie flat out in bed naked, dictating to her. She'll be propped up on pillows, her shorthand pad resting on her drawn-up legs. I think I'll be able to go straight through it, almost without a flaw, a glass of tequila at my left hand and my right hand occasionally straying to the notch between her thighs. And when the last word is taken down, we'll make love.

Surkov took the pad and pencil out of the girl's hands, and pulled her down to him. Their mouths met and clung, her thighs opened and he slid into her. When he had come, and moved gently away, the sky through the window was deep blue. They had tortillas and coffee in their room, brought up to them by the attractive black-eyed, barefoot Mexican girl.

In the cool of the evening they got dressed – she in jeans, T-shirt and sandals – and they wandered hand in hand on the edge of the dry desert, through the cactuses; and when they returned to the little hotel, the girl took down the last words of his story.

D·A·W·N

Go sleep with Turks and infidels . . .
SHAKESPEARE

It's time, my friend, it's time! the heart
is craving peace . . .
PUSHKIN

T·H·R·E·E

On the frontier between sleep and wakefulness, she was angry with her father because he had been so involved in Armenian politics he had had no time to teach her Armenian. Last night she had felt terribly ignorant; so many references she couldn't pick up. She hadn't even heard of Mickiewicz, though the Russian had said he was a great poet, whose talent for improvising had moved Pushkin to write *Egyptian Nights*. She had never heard of that work. The memory of her embarrassment reminded her that she had promised to make up an improvisation herself. She hoped the other two would have forgotten all about it. The poet from Moscow surely would have: he had got very drunk indeed, and developed a splitting head; he had staggered off with her bottle of aspirin, and his astonishingly loud snores had kept her awake for a long time.

She was ignorant. She was incapable, as her husband

always implied. But at least she was in Armenia! Excitement flooded through her again. Here, Haig didn't mean a hard-faced U.S. diplomat, but the founder of Armenia, his arrows aimed at Turkey, in righteous anger. She had been told that all the statues in the city were facing Turkey.

Khandjian came to her room soon after dawn had broken. He found her awake and dressed, waiting for him; waiting to be shown Ararat. On the plane from Moscow, a crew member had promised her, with a smile, that they would circle around Ararat just for her: since she was a long-lost, dark-skinned sister coming home! No longer Marian Fairfax, but Mariam Toumanian. . . . But darkness had fallen before Ararat could walk towards her; and she had only then recalled, ruefully, that it would have been impossible for a Soviet jet to circle Ararat, which was in a hostile country. She had astonished herself, at the airport in Yerevan, by kissing the soil.

He had anticipated having to waken her. It was not yet time to see Ararat. They talked in low voices. The hotel was silent. The Muscovite's snores had, over the past several hours, become deep, silent sleep. Mariam enquired if Aram had had much trouble in getting him to bed; and the mild-faced, pleasant Armenian replied that he had gone like a lamb; he had let him help him off with his clothes, had asked for a glass of water and a fresh packet of cigarettes; had apologized profusely for his agitation, his surliness, his boorishness, his maudlin fit of weeping; and wished him a kind good night. He did not want to be woken up to see Ararat before Yerevan's smog arose and veiled it, as Khandjian said it often did.

The Armenian, stockily built and short, dressed formally for the conference opening in a dark suit, white shirt and a tie, looked red-eyed and exhausted. He admitted he hadn't closed his eyes. He had attempted an improvisation, as a matter of fact: not because their Russian guest had been so drunkenly insistent, before his penitentially mild exit to bed, but because his snoring had prevented him from sleeping. He had started to wonder what was going on in the Russian's disturbed mind. Not that their unhappy friend – Khandjian glanced towards the wall – would recognize the portrait; but in any case he would not have the opportunity, for Khandjian had already wiped out the tapes. What had emerged had distressed and shocked him, he explained in answer to Mariam's disappointed query. He ought to have stuck to the ancient Armenian myths. He quoted the medieval poet Nareg, whose work Mariam did not know: "I created new misdeeds on top of the old. / And as Job said, made heavier the already unbearable weighty necklace . . . / Like a man with an unspellable name, I was erased / from the list of the census. / According to Esau, I became soiled / like a menstrual napkin. / And like an earthen dish / I was crushed beyond repair. . . ."

His cheeks became pink as he spoke the words "menstrual napkin." Mariam could picture him addressing students at Yerevan University. He would be very formal and correct. He taught Russian Literature, since – as he now explained to her – he preferred to keep private his deepest passion, for the great writers of Armenia.

He was walking about the room; and it only then occurred to her that he was waiting for her to invite him to sit down. Blushing, she did so belatedly; murmuring his thanks, he sat in a bedside chair. She was sitting on her bed, which she had made up while waiting for him to come.

They began to talk about the subject that had been too sacred to discuss in the presence of a non-Armenian: the holocaust and diaspora. And they discovered a coincidence which brought them very close in spirit. Their grandmothers had shared the forced march out of Kharput into the desert, in 1915; they had been among the hundred or so who had survived, out of many thousands. Khandjian's grandmother had actually been carrying a child – his mother, with whom he still lived – in her womb. Her young husband had been bayoneted to death at the outset of the march. She had given birth to the child in the Lebanon, and later moved with her to eastern Armenia, in its brief period of independence. His grandmother had never remarried, but had lived into her eighties – a splendid, fervently Christian old lady.

Mariam's grandmother had managed to get to the United States, eventually, with her two children – which was a miracle – but she also had left behind in Armenia the corpse of her husband. She had married again, in Massachusetts – another Armenian.

The next generation, Mariam's parents, had also been Armenian. She had broken the mould by marrying an Irish-American stockbroker. Her son was all-American.

Sharing the sorrows and miracles of their origins, the two Armenians spoke even more softly, and stretched towards each other; they caught hold of each other's hands. They confronted each other, like the twin peaks of Ararat. It seemed natural for him to move across and sit beside her on the bed; and natural that, finally, they should embrace each other. But Khandjian, who had never married and had had little experience of women, did not know whether to be pleased or alarmed when she let herself be persuaded to lie down with him.

He fumbled, in vain, at the buttons of her blouse. Blushing furiously, she moved into a sitting position, her back to him, and took off her blouse and bra, and then the rest of her clothes. She could hear him struggling out of his tight suit. She remembered to take out her contact lenses, cupping her hand to receive them. In her haste, she almost dropped a lens. She thought: If I stop to think, I'll back out of it. There had been little sex in her marriage, and no passion; even so, she had of course been faithful. But suddenly, unexpectedly, she wanted to be unfaithful. It had something to do with the feeling that she had come home, to a strange land. . . . Everything was new; and she, a virgin.

She turned, lay down again, and they embraced. They kissed and caressed each other for a long time; eventually he broke away from her — distressed, ashamed. She made light of it, kissing his lined forehead and stroking his wiry black hair. He was exhausted, she pointed out, and they were too much like brother and sister. Anyway, she was not very experienced at arousing men. He protested that this was nonsense: the fault was all his. He was no saint; he had had a relationship in Moscow when he had lived there for several years. There had been two or three other women there, more briefly. This had never happened before. Perhaps it was because she was Armenian, and married.

Well, she said, it was for the best. He was quite right: Armenian women should be faithful. He suggested they dress, and go to see Ararat. She agreed; yet the word "Ararat" suddenly held no charm for her. It turned to ash.

"Forgive me," he begged again; and she recognized in his tone and look a quality she found in herself, and in many Armenians: an enjoyment of humility. It enraged her. The more he apologized, the more she said it was just as well, the more it *wasn't* just as well. He was saying that he was still oppressed by the evil of his improvisation; and he quoted Nareg again: "Even if the seas change to salty ink, / and the forests of reeds are cut into pens / and the boundless fields spread with parchments / I could but finish writing a fraction / of my lawlessness. / And should I build a scales, / of the Cedars of Lebanon with Mount Ararat / on one side, my guilt would tilt the balance / to the other."

She licked her dry, thin lips, and her voice trembled as she said that he shouldn't blame himself too much. We were all a mixture of good and evil. Even his grandmother had obviously been capable of lying: for did he really imagine that she had borne an *Armenian*'s child, at the end of that march through the desert? . . . Then Khandjian, who had been perched on the side of the bed buttoning his shirt, turned on her, his face angry, took hold of her and thrust up into her, and she cried out, withdrawing her cruel words . . . Any Armenian woman raped by a Turk killed herself, if the Turk didn't kill her first. . . . But Khandjian, bearing down on her, continuing to thrust fiercely into her, said that it was true, she was right: his own response was proving it true. . . . Feeling that some demon had taken hold of her – perhaps by way of the Russian next door, who had disturbed her too – she let go completely of her Armenian and New England gentleness and cried, "Okay, it's true! You Turkish bastard! . . ."

"You Armenian bitch! . . ."

She caught hold of his hand and sank her teeth into the flesh, drawing blood; he exclaimed sharply, and called her a foul name in Armenian. "Yes," she said, "you can screw me now, can't you, you Turkish bastard, you mother-fucker! . . ."

Afterwards, lying quiet as a stone in his arms, she asked if there was anything else in Nareg, which might console her for her wickedness. "And mine," he said. "Especially mine." He thought for a while, and then said, "The very beginning of the *Lamentations*: 'My heart in plaintive lamentations sends up these sighs / toward you all secret-seeing God. / And the burning wish of my disturbed soul / is to scorch myself with the fire of grief . . .'"

"Even the foul words," she said: "I've never used them before. Forgive me."

He said: "It's all right. In spite of what we said and did, I feel very happy."

"So do I. It was my first experience of passion."

"Really? Not with your husband?"

"No. He's always made love to me as if I was the *Wall Street Journal* — with respect."

"Why don't you stay in Armenia?"

Her first impulse was to shake her head vehemently, because her thoughts flashed to her eighteen-year-old son. But then she said, "Well, why don't I?"

But she wouldn't say yes definitely. In fact she pretended her reply had been a joke. He professed disappointment at her back-tracking, while feeling secretly relieved. His proposal had frightened him.

But he asked her not to dismiss the suggestion out of hand, and she promised she wouldn't.

It was cooler. The heaviness of the night had lifted.

They took a shower together, laughing as they rubbed the foaming, soapy water into each other's bodies. He grew soapily erect under her sisterly hands, and wanted to make love to her again, in the shower; but she said no, she wished to see Ararat.

He took her up some stairs, to a landing window. At first she looked in the wrong direction; but he touched her shoulder and pointed her a little to the right; and she drew in her breath. There were the two snowy peaks, looking insubstantial, beyond the pink-stoned buildings of Yerevan, already turning golden in the morning light. And it was as a friendly Armenian had told her on the plane, when she had asked him how she would pick out Ararat from the whole range of mountains: "When you see it – you will know it. . . ."

She returned to her room while he went to rouse their drunken friend. He knew that, if their love-making had not woken him, knocking would not do it, so he walked straight in; and saw, almost at once, that the *improvisatore* was gone.

E·P·I·L·O·G·U·E

"THAT WAS WONDERFUL, SERGEI," OLGA SAID sleepily. "And so utterly different from your written work. Amazing! Thank you."

All night she had not stirred from the bed, nor interrupted the flow of his improvisation – except once, to go to the toilet.

Rozanov stood up from the armchair, yawned, and stretched his cramped limbs.

"What a dreadful man – Surkov."

"Ghastly!" Rozanov chuckled.

"I think I can guess who you were thinking of."

"Can you?"

The rain still lashed against the window, though the wind had quietened during the night. Dawn ought to have broken, but it was still pitch-dark in the room.

"It was amazingly controlled, Sergei. I just noticed one tiny error. Nothing, really. Colour blindness is mainly a confusion of red and green. So a lilac dress would be noticed."

"I know that," said Rozanov curtly. "But Charsky didn't."

"Ah, I see!"

They were silent, listening to the rain. Rozanov, who knew as little as Charsky about colour blindness, gazed at the green telephone in the murk, and wondered if the room might be bugged. He was conscious of having flirted with Russian roulette, and of having unforgivably involved others. Even the dumbest KGB man would know at once who "Kozarsky" stood for. It would be curtains for him: a convict train to the East. But the betrayal had slipped into the improvisation against Rozanov's will, when he had been half aware only of an urge to find himself bundled on to a plane to the West. . . . In effect, however, they would be more likely to reward him, for a subtle denunciation, than to punish him. . . . They'd probably give him a bigger *dacha*! A shudder ran down his spine. His only consolation was the certain knowledge that they would *not* have bugged a hotel room in Gorky. Olga would not say a word against him, and the references to Poland had passed over her head, he was sure.

The muscles of his head and neck relaxed. But that means nothing has changed, he reflected gloomily. There were advantages in living under the Green Frog. . . . (Ever since a noted professor, Zelenin, had vanished overnight from the *Great Soviet Encyclopaedia*, to be replaced by *zelenaya pyagushka* – "green frog" – Rozanov had privately referred to Stalin by that name.) All the same, he thought, how can I make amends for my stupid crime against a decent, honourable man? Perhaps I *will* call the

Sakharovs before I go, and wish them well. . . .

Olga was speaking to him, and he had to ask her to repeat it: a question about Surkov's attitude to women. "Don't forget the nice, quiet Armenian guy used him as a mouthpiece," he replied; "a scapegoat for his own evil imagination. 'For the imagination of man's heart is evil from his youth.' That's from the Bible. All we really know about the Russian poet is that he gets drunk and – slips across the border. Had they been able to compare their improvisations, as they had agreed, he would certainly have won, by a short head over the American lady. Of course he foresaw that he couldn't lose."

The curtained window had separated itself from the rest of the room, and Olga's naked breasts glimmered. Kolasky had woken up, he thought – soldiers woke early – and was screwing Sonia. And the bitch wouldn't even give him the satisfaction of admitting the affair outright, and sharing it with him. She maintained the fiction that she and the general were just friends, while knowing that he knew it was a fiction. Even the warning about Poland had been partly to goad him. When he had believed the affair might be over, her admission of an intimate exchange had driven him again into the frontier country between suspicion and certainty.

Well, he thought, with a sigh, I can't blame her. It's my own fault. What future can I offer her? I can't go through all that guilt and upset yet again. . . .

Olga broke into his thoughts by saying: "It seems a pity it can't be published, Sergei. Oh, I know some of it would have to be changed; but it was remarkable, truly."

"No, no. It's gone already. The text of last night does not exist. It has turned to stone, like the buried Armenian books. It has vanished like the two slave girls at the Fountain of the Palace of Bakhchisarai. Like Mardian's balls."

"I hope it hasn't *all* vanished. I certainly shall never forget it. It's been wonderful, wonderful. We shall meet again, shan't we? I'll come to Moscow, next time. I can easily make an excuse I've got to visit libraries."

"Well, that would be great."

"Come into bed, won't you? Make love to me."

He climbed into the narrow bed, and kissed her on the forehead. He explained that he was exhausted, and she said, "Of course, you *must* be. How selfish of me. Forgive me."

"I also feel a little shivery," he confessed. "I think I'm catching Surkov's fever."

Tenderly she rubbed his back, warming him, and he felt her blind eyes gazing down at him. After a time, he stopped shivering, but he confessed that he felt tense and highly strung. He often did after a performance.

"Can I do anything to help to relax you?" she asked.

"You're relaxing me already," he said. "But there's one thing that helps, though it will seem very stupid and childish. I've got into the habit lately of playing a TV game in the early morning, when I wake up. I've brought it with me. Do you mind if I plug it into the set?"

"No, of course not. What game is it?"

Rozanov climbed out of bed, fumbled in his overnight bag, then went to the small television. "It's pool," he said. "A kind of billiards. I got hooked when I went to America in the late Sixties. This TV game is based on it. It's American. A girl I once met over there sent me it."

He got back into bed, the control in his hand, and began

to send flashes of light across the grey screen. But he was too tired to play very well, and it wasn't much fun playing against himself. It was a pity the woman was blind. He recalled the girl in Sofia who had got really hooked on it, and played quite well; she had even beaten him a couple of times. They had sat up in bed, drinking coffee, eating rolls, absorbed in the battle on the screen. She'd been pretty good in bed too, Rozanov recalled.

With a deep screw he was able finally to finish the game off. Then as the woman, who still believed the game was continuing, gently stroked the hair on his chest, he turned his thoughts to the coming day. On the short flight he would correct the proofs of his essay on the spy and traitor Colonel Penkovsky. He would take Sonia to lunch, and if she was in a really good mood after a few glasses of vodka she might confess to a few caresses; and they would go back to her flat and make love. Yet, even if that happened, one couldn't be sure if she had, in reality, fucked all night or spent the evening and night entirely alone. He would drive back to Peredelkino in time to read Sasha his bedtime story; dine peacefully with his wife and perhaps have a game of chess with her. Then, when she had gone to bed, he would go to his study, draw the curtains against the night, and enjoy the rapture of silence and inspiration – his nape prickled at the very thought. . . . He would open the white book, pick up his pen; and, as madonnas and goddesses gazed down at him, he would go on with his long, secret poem about Meyerhold and his wife Zinaida.

Also available in ABACUS paperback:

FICTION

THE MONKEY KING	Timothy Mo	£2.75
SOUR SWEET	Timothy Mo	£2.95
TALES FROM THE DON	Mikhail Sholokhov	£2.95
WIDOWS	Ariel Dorfman	£2.25
NOBLE DESCENTS	Gerald Hanley	£2.95
GOOD BEHAVIOUR	Molly Keane	£2.95
THE SAFETY NET	Heinrich Böll	£2.95
A LONG WAY FROM VERONA	Jane Gardam	£2.25
MADAME SOUSATZKA	Bernice Rubens	£2.25

NON-FICTION

LETTERS FROM SACHIKO	James Trager	£2.75
THE SECOND STAGE	Betty Friedan	£2.95
KAFKA – A BIOGRAPHY	Ronald Hayman	£3.25
THE BAROQUE ARSENAL	Mary Kaldor	£2.95
SECRET POLICE	Thomas Plate & Andrea Darvi	£3.50
ROBERT GRAVES	Martin Seymour-Smith	£4.95
MRS HARRIS	Diana Trilling	£2.95
THE MAKING OF MANKIND	Richard Leakey	£5.95
IRELAND – A HISTORY	Robert Kee	£5.95

All Abacus books are available at your local bookshop or newsagent, can be ordered direct from the publisher. Just tick the titles you wa and fill in the form below.

Name _____

Address _____

_____

Write to Abacus Books, Cash Sales Department, P.O. Box 1 Falmouth, Cornwall TR10 9EN

Please enclose cheque or postal order to the value of the cover pri plus:

UK: 45p for the first book plus 20p for the second book and 14p for ea additional book ordered to a maximum charge of £1.63.

OVERSEAS: 75p for the first book plus 21p per copy for each additior book.

BFPO & EIRE: 45p for the first book, 20p for the second book plus 1 per copy for the next 7 books, thereafter 8p per book.

Abacus Books reserve the right to show new retail prices on cove which may differ from those previously advertised in the text elsewhere, and to increase postal rates in accordance with the PO.